NEVER FORGET

ECHO PLATOON SERIES
NOVELLA #2

MARLISS MELTON

A NOTICE TO THE READER/LIMIT OF LIABILITY/DISCLAIMER OF WARRANTY:

James-York Press
Williamsburg, Virginia

Edited by Sydney Jane Baily
Cover Design by Dar Dixon
Print Layout by BB Ebooks

ISBN-10: 1-938732-18-9
ISBN-13: 978-1-938732-18-8

DEDICATION

Having purchased this book, you have contributed to a very special place—a spiritual, physical, mental, and emotional retreat for Navy SEALs called LZ-Grace.

"LZ" stands for Landing Zone, as this is where SEALs can land after arduous, adrenaline-inducing, and terrifying operations. At LZ-Grace they can unwind in a wooded, creek-side environment. They benefit from meditation, massage, art and music therapy, and discussing experiences with those who have also lived through them. For all they do for us and for the free world, Navy SEALs deserve this special place. Thank you for contributing.

PROLOGUE

"SPEECH, SPEECH!" BELLOWED the SEALs sitting shoulder to shoulder in the rows of seats facing the raised platform. A warm June sun shone through the wall of windows and cast geometric shapes of light and shadow on their battle dress uniforms. Sweeping his dark gaze over his audience, Rusty Kuzinsky raised a hand to temper their exuberance.

The number of SEALs in attendance pleased him. It was a testament, he hoped, to the close connection he shared with "his boys"—though they weren't much more than a decade younger than he was.

Standing at the podium, he affirmed his earlier impression that every man in SEAL Team 12—not just those within his task unit—had packed into the Galley at the Dunes to attend his retirement ceremony. Maybe they just wanted a couple of hours away from Spec Ops. Maybe they just wanted to eat cake. But he would rather think it was because they would miss him.

His retirement ceremony had kicked off with the honor guard presenting the flags. Then a SEAL named Tristan Halliday had sung the national anthem. Commander Montgomery, aka Monty, had subsequently read the orders followed by a letter of thanks signed by the President himself. Monty then presented Rusty with a shadow box stuffed with the dozens of service medals and ribbons he'd earned in the last twenty-one years.

The team chaplain had taken over, reading a stirring poem about the American flag, while three junior SEALs folded a flag into a tight, neat triangle and presented it to him. After that, it was time for speeches. Monty could have offered up a decent tribute to him. But Rusty had a reputation for inspiring his boys, and they wanted a few last words of wisdom from him.

Reaching into the inner pocket of his dress whites, he withdrew several folded sheets of paper. "I actually wrote four different speeches," he admitted.

Laughter rolled through the sea of SEALs and echoed off the raftered ceiling of the ocean-side restaurant. They'd probably expected as much.

He smoothed the pages onto the podium while

deliberating which one to read.

"Just read 'em all, Master Chief," called a voice recognizable by its Montana drawl.

Casting Bronco an admonishing look, Rusty's gaze canted toward the blond-haired woman sitting next to him—not Rebecca, whom Bronco was due to marry next month, but NCIS Special Investigator Maya Schultz.

As their gazes locked, his thoughts short-circuited.

He hadn't seen Maya since last fall when he'd signed the paperwork declaring Bronco dead. It had all been part of an elaborate ploy on the part of NCIS to prove that Rusty's task unit leader was doing side jobs for the mob.

One look at Maya's piquant face and Rusty realized he'd been waiting all these months just to see her again.

Through the lenses of her plastic-framed glasses, her celadon-green gaze seemed to see into the deepest reaches of his soul—even from such a distance. Why would she have taken time away from work unless she felt the same way?

But then he remembered her late husband, who was dead because of him and his optimism waned.

Ian Schultz, a strapping Marine major, had died on Gilman's Ridge in a fateful battle that had taken the lives of thirty-two servicemen—every man but

Rusty, as a matter of fact. The running joke was he made too small of a target, though nothing to do with that day was a laughing matter.

Tearing his gaze from Maya's, he pulled himself up to every one of his five feet, six inches and looked back at his speeches. Maya Schultz's expectant gaze had him pushing all the pages to one side.

"You know, I never really thought this day would happen," he admitted.

Glancing up, he took a mental snapshot of the expectant faces gazing back at him. A wave of affection rolled over him tightening his vocal cords.

"I've been a SEAL since I was nineteen. That's twenty-one years of HALO jumps, firefights, and ordinance disposal. That's seven tours—five in Afghanistan and two in Venezuela. Going by the numbers, I shouldn't have made it this far. But I did, and it's thanks to those who lost their lives fighting alongside me."

He raised his gaze to the room's periphery, where the ghosts who haunted him day and night seemed to hover. His knuckles ground against the sharp edges of the podium as he grounded himself in reality.

Glancing back at his notes, he looked over the names he had listed the previous day. "Please stand while I acknowledge the men who made this day possible."

With a rustle of canvas and the scuffing of boots on the tiled floor, his audience rose respectfully. Out the corner of his eye, Rusty lost sight of Maya Schultz, whose diminutive stature caused her to disappear behind the broad shoulders of the SEALs in front of her.

Reading one name at a time, Rusty memorialized the fallen warriors with whom he'd served. When he came to Ian Schultz's name, he gave it special emphasis. *I'm sorry I couldn't save him,* he mentally projected.

Coming to the last name, he looked up to find his men's eyes misted over. "To all of these fallen, to my wise leaders, and to you, my boys, I give you my sincerest thanks."

It took a second for the SEALs to throw off the somber pall he'd cast over them. A subdued applause moved through the audience.

"Thanks for coming," he added. "Now let's eat cake."

The response this time was unanimous. "Hooyah, Master Chief!"

As the aisles began to clear, Rusty put away his notes while trying to catch a glimpse of Maya's reaction. Had she appreciated his recognition of her late husband? Would she consent to see him if he called on her?

The sight of her blond curls headed toward the exit brought his head sharply around.

Wait. He barely caught himself from calling her back.

The door thudded shut behind her, and a stark emptiness welled up in him, pulling him into a familiar undertow of guilt. What had he expected—that just because he'd recognized her husband publically, he deserved forgiveness?

"Well done, Rusty." The Commander of SEAL Team 12 stood next to him offering a handshake. Joe Montgomery's shadowed eyes and scarred face reflected a shared sense of suffering.

"Thank you, sir."

"I hear you've got plans for that big old house you've renovated."

"Yes, sir." Never Forget Retreat sat on thirty-three acres of pine forest and salt-water marsh. He hoped it would offer special operators fresh out of overseas assignments a refuge in which to put their hearts and minds back together before reintegrating into normal life.

"It's commendable what you're doing, Rusty. I could have used a place like that once."

The words reminded Rusty that the CO had survived a catastrophe that had taken the lives of all his teammates.

"We all could have, sir. That's why I created it."

Monty clapped him on the shoulder. "You don't have to call me sir anymore," he said with a crooked smile. "Now come cut your cake," he ordered good-naturedly.

CHAPTER ONE

"C URTIS!"

Hearing frustration in her own voice as she hollered upstairs to her teenage son, Maya backed up and returned to the kitchen for a second impression. Maybe it wasn't as bad as she'd first thought.

It was worse.

She hadn't seen the sticky-looking spill on the linoleum floor on her first pass. Of course, the spill would account for all the empty glasses by the sink and the empty bottle of sweet tea on the island. Crumbs littered the countertop. The loaf of bread— or what remained of it—had been left out to go stale. Knives coated in mustard and mayonnaise lay atop the crumbs, and an empty bag of chips perched precariously atop the overflowing trash bin.

Over the rapid thudding of her heart, Maya made out several teenage voices coming from the second story which explained the array of empty glasses and the reason the bread was almost gone. Curtis had friends over—despite their rule that no friends were allowed while she was at work. And certainly not without prior permission.

Pressing her palm to her forehead, she drew a steadying breath and then another.

If only Ian were still here.

For more than a decade, that litany had played through her head like a broken record. She had thought the phrase would cease to be apropos—eventually. But instead of growing more at peace with Ian's death, the older Curtis got, the more she resented her husband's absence. At fourteen, her son was already proving more than she could handle. Having Ian around would have made all the difference.

Curtis's age was only half the problem. Now that school was out for the summer, he had way too much time on his hands and no structure. Too young to go to work and too old to go to affordable camps, he hung out at home or with neighborhood kids instead of the "nice" kids that attended his private school—a luxury she scrimped to pay for. Here it was, only the first part of June and he was breaking the rules already.

Bracing herself for battle, she dumped the bag of groceries she still clutched in one arm onto the counter and marched up the stairs.

No wonder he hadn't heard her calling. The sounds of a violent video game penetrated Curtis's closed door. With an indrawn breath, she turned the doorknob and quietly pushed it open.

If she'd thought the kitchen was trashed, then there were no words to describe the mess before her. Four adolescent boys glanced distractedly in her direction before turning their focus back to the game.

"Hey, Mom," Curtis said, managing to acknowledge her.

Maya counted to ten. Then, drawing herself to her fullest height, she marched in front of the huge computer monitor Curtis had moved from the family room to his bedroom, reached down, and pushed the power button.

"What the hell?" one of Curtis's friends, larger than any fourteen-year-old should be, exclaimed loudly.

She sent the boy a look that had made many a guilty serviceman confess to his crimes, yet he scarcely blinked. "I'm sorry," she announced, then wished she hadn't started with an apology. "You're all going to have to leave right now."

"What?" Curtis lowered his controller. "Mom, you can't be serious!"

"Oh, I'm perfectly serious." She glanced toward

the three boys whom she only vaguely recognized. The big one with the smart mouth lounged on Curtis's beanbag chair like he had no intention of going anywhere.

She took a step in his direction. "I don't believe we've been introduced." She glanced pointedly at Curtis.

"That's Santana," he mumbled.

The boy must have been taught some manners a long time ago because he came to his feet, albeit with a look of annoyance. He towered over her, looking about sixteen years old, and did not extend his hand.

"Santana," she repeated. Her gaze slid from the resentful curl on his upper lip, to the stained T-shirt, to the baggy jeans hanging on his narrow hips. She offered hers first. "Hi, I'm Curtis's mom, Mrs. Schultz." He supplied a limp handshake.

"Unfortunately," she said, repulsed by the feel of his sticky fingers, "Curtis does not have permission to have friends over while I'm at work." She sent Santana a tight smile. *So you can leave now,* she silently conveyed.

His derisive gaze drifted over her, taking in her smart, cream-colored suit, bare calves, and three-inch heels. "You're here now, ain't you?" he pointed out.

His insolence stripped the air from her lungs but

only for a second. "Yes, I am here," she said, in a voice underlined by steel. "But Curtis is now grounded so, not only can't you play here, but you won't be able to come back anytime soon."

"Oh, come on, Mom." Curtis's protest faded at the withering look she sent him. "All right, guys. You gotta go." Rolling to his feet, he shepherded his friends out of his bedroom and down the stairs.

Maya followed at a distance, rehearsing the words she was going to say while searching for the level-headedness she was famous for at work. But her blood kept boiling, forcing her to acknowledge that she was furious—not so much at Curtis as at fate.

Why couldn't Ian have survived that fateful firefight on Gilman's Ridge? Why couldn't he have retired today like Master Chief Kuzinsky had that afternoon? And why couldn't she get that economy-sized power-pack of a SEAL out of her head?

That instant she'd laid eyes on him, a feeling akin to joy had blossomed in her before she'd squashed it. She hadn't felt that way about a man since ... since Ian. And even though Ian had been dead for more than a decade, finding Kuzinsky attractive was just plain wrong.

He and his platoon had been sent up Gilman's Ridge to rescue the Marines. Yet within forty-eight hours, every jarhead and frogman alike had ended up dead—every man but Rusty, who seemed to have a near-miraculous talent for survival.

It wasn't fair to say he was responsible for Ian's death but—yes—it was easier to blame him than to admit that some part of her that had lain dormant since Ian came home in a casket fluttered like a butterfly in Rusty's uber-masculine presence.

Besides that, she admired his disciplined and self-restrained mannerisms, his intelligence, and his loyalty to his subordinates. The fact that his underlings held him in such high esteem said something for him, too. However, his mentioning Ian at his retirement ceremony had stung like salt in an old wound. It had left her feeling guilty for finding the SEAL so compelling.

The front door gave a slam, wresting Maya from her tortuous thoughts. Curtis stormed into the kitchen and glared at her, his arms akimbo.

"Thanks a lot," he growled, flicking the overlong blond bangs out his eyes. "Now they're probably not going to play games here anymore because they think my mom is a bitch."

She noted the obscenity with rising fury. "I don't care what they think of me. You know the rules and you flouted them. Now you have to face the consequences. You're grounded for a week, and I never want to find out that your so-called friends have been in my house while I'm away."

He sneered at her warning. "You don't know anything about my friends."

"No, I don't. I don't know what their names are, who their parents are, or whether they're a good influence or not. And until I do, they're not to come here. I can tell you right now that Santana is trouble, and you need to stay away from him."

"You can't tell me who my friends should be."

"That's my job, actually."

"Well, I don't think so. Stop treating me like I'm some stupid military person who broke the rules and has to go to jail."

"I'm not. I'm treating you like a fourteen-year-old who's getting too big for his britches. Now clean up this kitchen and then you can start on your bedroom while I cook our supper."

As he drew a shuddering breath, his expanding chest took on the burly dimensions he would eventually grow into, inherited from his father. A frisson of alarm shot to the ends of Maya's fingertips. What if he grew too large and rebellious for her to handle?

If only Ian were still here.

"Fine," he snarled, relieving her for the time being. But then he wheeled toward the wall closest to him and punched it—hard.

Maya gaped, not believing that her son had just plowed his fist into the wall. But there was no mistaking the impression of Curtis's knuckles as he snatched his hand back and wheeled away, rubbing his bruised flesh and hissing with discomfort.

"Well that's one more thing that will need fixing," she pointed out before turning away and stalking to her bedroom to change her clothing. "You can put away the groceries I bought while you're cleaning up," she tossed over her shoulder.

Closing and locking her door, she threw herself across her bed, hugged a pillow to her chest, and stared sightlessly at the painting hanging next to her bed—a watercolor of a smiling Ian she'd commissioned after his death. She'd been determined to keep him in her thoughts, a part of her life no matter what.

Funny, but when she stared at his face while lying horizontal, he looked a bit like Rusty Kuzinsky who also kept his hair cut short—except Rusty's hair was auburn where Ian's had been chestnut. Both men had brown eyes, though Rusty's were darker, like twin ponds at night. They seemed to hold the most profound thoughts.

Bronco had told her that, following retirement, Rusty was starting up a retreat where active duty SEALs could recuperate following especially tough assignments. He wanted to help them exorcise their demons, to heal and adjust to peacetime before returning to their families.

Ian could have used a place like that. He'd always been so jumpy and irritable his first few weeks back from an overseas tour.

Rusty's charity only added to all the appealing traits she'd noted about him. It made her feel shallow for holding a grudge against him all these years. How could she resent a man who considered the welfare of others to such an extent that he shaped his life's purpose around it?

But if she forgave him completely, then this shroud in which she'd lain dormant might become something like a cocoon, transforming her into something altogether new. Change was frightening. It was safer to stay the way she was, clinging to bitterness, and raising her rebellious son as best she could.

CHAPTER TWO

MOVING FROM ROOM to room in the eight-bedroom farmhouse he'd restored, Rusty jotted down the items still requiring his attention.

In just five days, his first lodgers would arrive—members of SEAL Team 3, home-based in Coronado. They would stay at Never Forget Retreat for two weeks before returning home. This place would be their halfway house—a place to shed the mantle of war, to calm an overly responsive nervous system, and to begin feeling human again.

Taking in all that he'd done, Rusty basked in self-satisfaction. The bedrooms, painted in manly blues, greens, and grays, invited occupants to take their rest on the brand-new mattresses all donated by companies around Virginia Beach.

Most of the furniture was second hand, but he had an eye for what styles and eras went with what—traditional with contemporary, antique with retro-chic. All those nights of lowering the blinds so he could watch the Home and Garden channel in secret had apparently paid off. From the pillows tossed on inviting armchairs to the bedding and artwork, each room felt like a place to find rest.

With his small checklist started, Rusty headed down the front staircase, pleased when the treads didn't give even the tiniest squeak. On the lower level, he'd removed many of the original walls to create an open-concept floor plan.

A large parlor with a piano original to the house funneled guests from the foyer toward the living area and then to the farm-style kitchen that occupied the addition at the rear of the house. French doors on the right side of the living area led to an expansive sunporch with wicker furniture and potted plants.

Sweeping stairs bisected the house, leaving room at the front for an enclosed library with built-in bookcases overflowing with books on every subject. To the rear, the formal dining room with its Italian-style table and high-backed chairs offered seating for up to twenty. Rusty had contracted with two different cooks to whip up meals daily—though, truth be told, he wished he could do the cooking himself.

Of course, he would be too busy arranging activities for the men to have time to cook. SEALs were used to having a constant objective. Lounging around doing nothing wouldn't cut it. Thus, Rusty stored an arsenal full of paintball guns and a fleet of used all-terrain vehicles in the barn beside the house—all donated by patriotic store owners who'd responded to his appeals.

He had diving equipment for anyone wanting to swim up the creek to the sound, cornhole equipment, a permanent volleyball net out back, and plans to build an obstacle course.

His neighbors, the Digges family, owned a stable full of horses and offered trail rides at discounted prices should Rusty's guests show any interest. The trails in the woods offered long walks and fresh air and a place to play war games. And the creek offered ample opportunity to catch catfish or go crabbing.

In addition to the cooks who would come in daily, Rusty had partnered with local artists, musicians, writers, counselors, and wellness experts—scheduling them to visit the men, illustrating various ways of coping with the horrors branded in their minds, either from their most recent tour or from an accumulation of their military experience.

I'm almost ready, he assured himself. All he needed were the few crowning touches that he had jotted onto his note pad.

Crossing to the piano, he trilled the recently-tuned keys while surveying the lower level with a critical eye. Ah, yes. The door to the powder room reminded him. He still needed a trash bin in there—off-white metal with a raised design to match the framed prints hanging on the beige walls.

The sound of a vehicle barreling up his dirt driveway had him spinning toward the window in anticipation of a hostile force. Of course, there was no enemy. But beyond the front porch with its assortment of colorful rockers, a black, government issued SUV kicked up dust in its haste to reach his house.

Behind a tinted windshield, he made out a youthful and unfamiliar face. The SUV braked, and the driver, dressed in fatigues, leaped out from behind the steering wheel, slamming his door shut. With a harried glance at the back of his SUV, he hurried toward Rusty's front door.

What the hell is this about?

With a thought for the Gerber blade hidden under his pant leg, Rusty went to answer the man's sturdy knock. Years of service in faraway, dangerous places made him cautious when opening a door, but the young man's earnest gaze banished his concerns right away.

"Master Chief Kuzinsky?"

Given the desperation oozing out of the young man, Rusty knew an impulse to deny his identity. "Retired," he said, glancing at the patches on the man's BDU jacket. Apparently, he was a marine sergeant with the last name of Mata.

Rusty's retirement was clearly news to the jar-head. "Oh, congratulations," he said.

"How can I help you?" Rusty asked.

Sergeant Mata gestured toward his vehicle and that's when Rusty heard it—the unmistakable bark of a Belgian Malinois—grating, persistent, like an intermittent alarm going off. "I've brought you the service dog you asked for."

Rusty's brain short-circuited for the second time in two days.

"I never asked for a service dog." He stepped back tempted to close the door in the man's face.

Sergeant Mata frowned down at his paperwork. "But you did," he insisted. "Back in 2012, you left a request at Lackland asking to get Draco when he was retired from service."

"Draco?" With a feeling like he'd been kicked in the gut, Rusty looked back at the black SUV. "That's Draco in there?"

"Yes, Master Chief—I mean, sir. He's nine now, too old for another tour. My orders say you signed up to adopt him if anything happened to his handler."

"Nichols," Rusty breathed, naming Draco's handler. "What happened?"

Mata shook his head. "He was killed two weeks ago. Explosives were buried deep under the road, and Draco didn't catch the scent."

Nichols' youthful face and ready smile panned through Rusty's mind, memories snagging on his heart and tearing through it.

"It wasn't the dog's fault," the soldier defended the military war dog. "He should've been retired years ago. He was just so good at what he did."

Rusty had to clear his throat to find his voice. "What about Draco. Was he hurt?"

"He was caught at the edge of the blast. It concussed him but he's okay now, as you can hear."

What Rusty heard was sixty pounds of frustration. He *so* did not need a dog right now. But Sergeant Mata's expression spoke of sheer dread at the thought of returning Draco to wherever they'd come from—all the way from Lackland? What's more Rusty made a point of honoring his obligations. He couldn't back out on this one, just because the timing wasn't great.

"I guess he's my dog, then." Resignation vied with a tingle of excitement. "Go ahead and bring him in."

The relief that lit up the sergeant's face assured Rusty that he'd done the right thing. He stepped out onto the veranda, watching while the sergeant went back to the SUV and opened the rear hatch. The dog was obviously crated inside. Mata reached in to unlatch the crate, and a tornado exploded out of the

SUV, sailing over the man's shoulder and landing in the driveway where it took off like a shot for the tree line.

"Draco!" Mata yelled, watching him go while holding an empty leash in his hands.

Ho, boy.

It'd been four years since Rusty had watched Nichols work with the dog, but he distinctly remembered the way the handler called him. Good thing Rusty could whistle the same way.

The instant his high-pitched, lilting call carried across the yard, the dog screeched to a halt, lifted his leg on a bush, then trotted steadily toward Rusty, his gaze watchful, tongue hanging out the side of his mouth.

At the bottom of the steps, the dog abruptly halted, staring up at him and panting hard.

Rusty squatted and held out a hand. "Hey, Draco," he crooned. "Remember me, buddy?"

The dog's tall, pointed ears swiveled in his direction. He closed his mouth to scent the air. Sergeant Mata had frozen, watching with a hopeful expression.

Returning the intelligent brown gaze of the dog resembling a small German Shepherd, Rusty was struck by how war had aged the animal. His coat was still more black than caramel. The eyebrows that looked painted-on still gave him an expressive appearance. But a hint of silver lightened his dark muzzle, and the wild look in his eyes reminded Rusty of the way veteran SEALs looked fresh off the battlefield.

Hell, he'd seen that look staring back at him in a bathroom mirror.

Draco needed this place as much as the next war-weary operator.

"It's me, Draco. *Hier,*" he said, calling him over with the Dutch command Nichols had used.

The dog's eyes turned liquid. His ears flattened. Breathing fast, he padded up the steps to bump Rusty's outstretched hand while sniffing him. Suddenly, his whole body began to wag. Rearing up on his hind legs, he planted his forepaws on Rusty's shoulders and knocked him off his feet, pinning him flat on the porch while licking his face in delighted recognition.

"I think he remembers you," Sergeant Mata drawled, having made his way closer.

The urge to laugh tightened Rusty's vocal cords. He wanted to wrestle with the dog, show him who was alpha, except he didn't trust the dog not to bite. Better to build up the bonds of trust first.

"*Los,*" he said, ordering the dog to release him. Squirming out from under him, he grabbed Draco's collar and clambered to his feet. "Better come inside," he said to the sergeant, "if you want me to sign that paperwork."

RUSTY SLIT HIS eyes open in order to read the clock beside his bed. It was two in the morning, and this was the third time he'd been wakened, this time by an unidentifiable noise.

At twenty-one hundred, he'd put Draco in the barn for the night, but the dog hadn't stayed there. Incessant barking had seen him transferred almost immediately to the house. Rusty had shut him up in the bathroom downstairs, where barking had turned into howling.

He'd then brought the dog upstairs and put him inside his closet. Draco had fallen silent, seemingly content, and Rusty had crawled back into bed, shoved wax earplugs into his ears, and gone back to sleep.

But this noise that he'd awakened to wasn't one he readily recognized. Prying a plug out of one ear, he came wide awake as it occurred to him it was a *gnawing* sound. Oh, shit, the dog was eating his way out of the closet.

"No!" Vaulting out of bed, Rusty threw open the closet door, startling the dog who shrank back into the far corner. Groping for the nearest light switch, Rusty flinched against the glare even as he leaned into the large closet to assess the damage.

Sure enough, the dog had done his damnedest to get out of his makeshift quarters. Part of the trim and a large segment of the drywall lay in soggy pieces on the closet floor. And here Rusty had thought Draco was happy simply to be close to him.

A vision of the dog nestled next to Nichols' legs came to him belatedly. Draco was used to sleeping in the same bed with his handler, his chin resting on Nichols' thigh.

Meeting the glassy gaze of the frightened canine, Rusty cursed himself.

"My fault, boy," he admitted. Sinking into a crouch, he held out a hand.

"Draco, *hier*. You're not in trouble. I forgot what you were used to, that's all. It's been a long time since I've been played in the sandbox," he added, remembering Afghanistan by the name service people used for it. "Don't like to think about it, actually."

The dog sniffed his hand, mistrustful at first but responsive to his conversational tone.

"Bet you didn't like the sandbox either. Or maybe you did—lots to do there, huh? Bet you miss Nichols." Pain pegged Rusty's chest as the dog's ears swiveled forward. "You still recognize his name," he realized.

Sorrow swamped him abruptly, and he rolled onto one hip to stroke the soft plane between Draco's ears. The dog submitted, lowering his head to the floor. Then he elbow-crawled forward to put his chin on Rusty's knee.

Touched by the gesture of trust, Rusty let himself remember as he caressed the dog from his head to his haunches. He pictured Nichols in the mess tent piling bacon and sausage on top of his eggs. Nichols taking point with Draco. He'd walked way ahead of them, putting himself and the dog between the Navy SEALs and certain death. Rusty remembered Nichols writing long letters to his wife, showing him pictures of his two girls.

And now the man was dead. His wife left without a husband. Those girls were growing up without a father. And Draco's world had imploded.

A too-familiar pain knifed Rusty's heart. He found himself picturing Maya Schultz, whose heart-shaped face was still fresh in his mind from the other day. Ten years had passed since her husband's death, and she still hadn't gotten over it. He could tell by the way she looked at him, like she couldn't believe he'd let her husband die.

The fact that she blamed him—not in an active way, but subconsciously—that hurt.

If she only knew how desperately he had fought—how they'd all fought to stay alive. If she only knew how many times he'd wished he could have died in someone's stead—anyone's.

The sensation of a tear sliding down his cheek brought him back to the present. Looking down, he found Draco asleep with his chin on Rusty's knee. Suddenly he knew what the dog needed. Hell, maybe he needed it, too. He shifted, and Draco's eyes slowly opened.

"Come on, buddy. Let's get in bed." He pushed to his feet and snapped off the light.

Ignoring his slight abhorrence at the thought of having a dog in his bed—all that hair—, he slipped back under the covers and patted the space beside him. "*Hier.*"

The dog bounded onto the bed next to him, turned in a circle three times, and collapsed onto the comforter.

Rusty found his fingers sifting through the dog's soft fur. His eyes closed. The breath flowed in and out of his lungs like waves, rolling and retreating.

He would rather have a woman in his bed than a dog. And not just any woman.

A vision of Maya Schultz curling up next to him sent a shaft of longing through him.

What would she think about sharing her bed with a man and a dog? Considering she blamed the man for her husband's death, the question was probably a moot one. He'd never find out.

He could dream, though, couldn't he?

CHAPTER THREE

M AYA STARED AT the array of wall plaster in Home Depot, wondering if any one brand was better than the others. She hadn't owned a house since she sold the one Ian and she had bought as newlyweds. She had rented ever since, so that things like broken hot water heaters and burst pipes were her landlord's problem and not hers. But telling her latest landlord about the dent in the wall was out of the question. She would fix it herself and paint over the fresh plaster and none would be the wiser. But which brand to choose?

If only Ian were still here.

Grabbing the tub that looked the most familiar, she glanced behind her at the distinct sound of panting. The sight of a dog standing two feet away staring at her rocked her back on her heels. On the other end of his leash stood Rusty Kuzinsky, whose dark gaze hit her like a mainlined methamphetamine.

Oh, my God. Had she conjured him by thinking of him so much?

"Hello," he said. He sent her a suggestion of a smile that crinkled the corners of his eyes and made him look ten years younger. And so damn attractive that her insides seemed to melt.

"Hi." Her heart started to bounce against her breastbone. Could he tell?

"Need some help?" He glanced at the tub of putty in her hands and then back into her eyes.

"Oh. Um." And now she was stammering. "Actually, I think I'm okay."

The dog stretched out his neck in an attempt to sniff at her shorts.

"*Zit,*" Rusty said, and the dog immediately sat.

Maya blinked and looked up, wondering what language that was.

"Filling in holes in your walls?" he asked, glancing back at the tub.

"A dent," she admitted. She looked back at the dog. "Who's this?" Maybe if they focused on the dog, her pulse would stop racing.

"My newest problem," Rusty said on a note of irony. "Years ago, I volunteered to adopt him when he was retired from service."

She regarded the dog with fresh eyes. "A military dog. That explains why he's so well-behaved."

He issued a laugh that made her think of sandpaper. "He's not that well behaved," he assured her.

"No?"

"No." His ruddy lips twitched toward a smile that made her wonder what kissing him would feel like.

"I guess he could be," he qualified. "But like any warrior just off the field of battle, he's still pretty keyed up. I spent the whole morning running him when I have better things to do." He glanced at the display. "In fact, I'm going to need a tub of that to patch the damage he did last night."

"Oh dear." She moved over so he could make his selection.

"So, what's your boy doing with himself this summer?" he asked as he stepped alongside her.

She caught a whiff of lemon and sage and...dog.

"Oh, Curtis is just hanging around the house," she admitted.

At her cool tone, Rusty turned his head to regard her inquiringly.

"School's out." He heard her add, "And he's fourteen now—too young to work and too old for the camp he attended last year. His school friends all live pretty far away, so he's been hanging out with some bad elements in our neighborhood." She shrugged. "I'm just not sure what to do with him."

Rusty's onyx gaze plumbed her own. She wet her lips wishing she had put on makeup that morning.

"Did he put that dent in the wall?"

The quiet question turned her mouth dry. Was he psychic or something?

"With his fist?" he added.

She found she couldn't lie with him watching her reaction. "Well, yes, but it's the first time he's ever done anything like that," she assured him.

His gaze slid down and to the right. "Bet you tell yourself things would be different if your husband were still alive."

The words stopped her heart momentarily. He had to be psychic. How could he know that?

As he looked up again, she closed her mouth, which had fallen open.

"Tell you what." His lips firmed and his freckled forehead furrowed as he mulled over whatever it was he was about to say.

She realized she was holding her breath.

"What if I gave your son a job?"

Her thoughts went to the big old house he'd renovated as a retreat for active-duty SEALs. "What kind of job?" It was probably her fault, but her son was as unskilled at fixing things as she was.

He gestured to the dog, which had stood up restlessly, apparently recalled he was supposed to be sitting, and sat down again. "Playing with my dog."

Maya regarded the animal with reservation. Between his dark coloring and his fierce, military aspect, he looked dangerous. "Isn't that a bit risky? Military dogs are notoriously aggressive—they have to be."

"True," he conceded. He thought for a second, averting his gaze. "But he's used to being with a handler 24/7, and his was killed a short while back."

His tone of voice also conveyed that he'd known the handler. "I'm so sorry," she said. She regarded the orphaned dog with sympathy.

"I could use Curtis to take Draco for long walks, throw the ball, and generally hang out with him while doing stuff for me like clearing paths in the woods."

A vision of Curtis spending time outdoors teased her imagination. "Aren't you expecting company soon?" she asked.

Rusty just looked at her. "Bronco tell you that?"

"He told me about the retreat, yes. I think it's a wonderful project." She let her admiration warm her tone.

"Then you can see why I don't have time to work with this dog."

"Yes, but my boy's only fourteen. And we've never had a dog." Curtis had always wanted one, though.

"Let's try it on a trial basis," he proposed. "I can pick up Curtis in the morning before you go to work. He'll stay with me until you come get him when your workday's over."

"Are you sure?" He was willing to put up with a teenager for hours on end? "You've never had children, have you?"

That same sandpaper laugh escaped him, causing her stomach to flip at how attractive it sounded. "I've had nieces and nephews and a few SEALs who were still teenagers, but no. No kids of my own."

"You might not realize what you're getting into," she warned.

"That's the reason for the trial basis."

She blew out a breath, deliberating. "Okay." She spread her hands and shrugged. "Let's try it."

"Great." His ruddy lips twitched toward a smile. He handed her a pen and index card which he produced from his thigh pocket. "What time and where?"

She turned the card over, noting his neatly written shopping list. "Is eight thirty too early?" she asked.

"Nope."

Jotting down her address she had to quell the tremor in her fingertips at the prospect of seeing him again Monday morning.

"If you change your mind after you meet him, it won't hurt my feelings," she promised handing him back the card and pen.

He studied her address a moment and then

looked at her. "Do you think he's going to like the idea?"

"Probably not," she admitted, "but it beats being grounded." She sent him a tight smile.

"Ah," he said. Private thoughts flickered in his dark eyes sparking her curiosity to know what they were. "I'll see you in two days then. What time in the afternoon will you pick him up?"

"Well, I've cut back on my hours for the summer so I'm off at three."

"Perfect. It'll take you fifteen minutes from the air base to get to this address." Handing her a business card, he pointed out the address on it.

His efficiency impressed her. He'd been the same way during the investigation of his commander last fall, deftly handling everything needed to prove his leader's unethical ties to the mob. No wonder he'd risen so high in the enlisted ranks.

She took note of his obscure address—Muddy Creek Road, Pungo. "Good thing I have GPS."

"It's a straight shot down Virginia Beach Boulevard."

"I'll find it," she promised him. "Should I pack Curtis a lunch?"

"Oh, no. I'll feed him."

"Thank you. He'll eat anything you give him."

"Plus I'll pay him five an hour. It's not even minimum wage but it'll add up."

"Oh, you don't have to do that." She ought to be paying *him* for getting her son out of the house.

"He'll need the incentive," he said with assurance.

Picturing Curtis's response to the new arrangement, he was probably right. "Okay," she agreed. She nodded at the putty in his hand. "Good luck with the repairs."

"Same to you," he said.

Conscious of the shy smile on her face, she backed up three steps before whirling and walking briskly away from him. She could feel his gaze burning a warm path down her back, and she found herself putting a subtle sway in her step, wondering if he found her bare legs pretty.

At the end of the aisle, she glanced back just as he jerked his gaze up. Their eyes met again and a fresh wave of heat rushed into her cheeks, causing her to blush like a school girl. She darted out of sight to hide her flustered state.

WHAT THE HELL have I done?

Reality slapped Rusty from his trance as Maya turned the corner. Clearly, his brain became mush in her presence. There was no other explanation for the fact that he'd just saddled himself with another responsibility—like the dog wasn't enough of a handful. Now he had to keep an eye on her son, too.

What had he been thinking?

Sure, the kid could throw the ball and take the dog for long hikes in the woods. But he'd lied about Draco not being dangerous. Any Navy SEAL dog worth his salt loved to bite. The more aggressive, the more type-A, the more capable a dog was of protecting his teammates. War dogs weren't your average domesticated canine. And they didn't turn sweet and cuddly overnight—especially not Belgian Malinois, who'd been bred for centuries to be high-strung, fearless, and aggressive.

Crap. If Rusty didn't take the time to train both boy and dog, the kid was going to get some puncture wounds. And then Maya Schultz wouldn't even speak to him, let alone want to know him better. So why the new arrangement?

Scrubbing a hand across his forehead, he envisioned the vulnerability he'd glimpsed on her face when she admitted that her son had plowed his fist into the wall.

Yep, it was that helpless look that did it. The only thing worse than her son getting bitten by his dog on his property was the prospect of the kid unleashing his frustration on his mother in their own home, where no adult male was present to protect her.

I am such a pushover.

Draco got up and started walking. Sixty pounds of determination dragged Rusty in the direction of the exit.

"And we're done shopping," he acknowledged.

At least he'd gotten what he came for—plus a whole lot more. All that responsibility for what? For the unlikely prospect of forging a connection with the widow of one of his fallen teammates. He sneered at his uncharacteristic optimism.

Good luck.

CHAPTER FOUR

MAYA MARCHED INTO her son's bedroom and raised the shade, admitting brilliant morning sunshine. "You need to get up *now*, honey. He'll be here in twenty minutes."

Curtis pulled the pillow over his eyes. "Why?" he whined in a voice that started in a boy's register and broke into a man's.

He'd been asking that same question—*Why?*—ever since she'd informed him that come Monday he'd be working for a retired Navy SEAL, helping to care for the military dog he'd just adopted.

"I don't want this stupid job," he added.

Ignoring his protest, she grabbed his blanket and pulled it off him. The length of his growing, half-naked body drove home just how big he was getting. It was about time he took on more responsibility.

"You're going to love it," she predicted. "You've been asking me for a dog for years. This will be just like having one—and you'll be paid, too. So up and at 'em. Time to roll," she added, using one of Ian's favorite expressions and employing his brook-no-arguments tone of voice.

She'd been thinking of Ian a lot lately. If not Ian, then Rusty.

"Fine." Curtis dragged himself to a sitting position and swung his feet to the floor. "How long do I have to do this?"

"I don't know," she said, relieved that he was finally cooperating. "As long as it lasts, I guess."

"All summer?" He plodded into his bathroom while wiping the sleep from his eyes.

"I don't know," she repeated as he shut the door between them.

What did she hope to get out of the arrangement, besides the peace of mind in knowing Curtis was gainfully occupied while she was at work? A vision of Rusty's dark eyes, his ruddy lips curving toward a smile caused her pulse to accelerate. Did she want to get to know him better?

Yes. What would Ian have thought of him?

She didn't know. He'd never mentioned Rusty Kuzinsky, probably hadn't even known him before that fateful day on Gilman's Ridge. So many men slaughtered in an attempt to save just one.

Shaking off the memory, she left the room to finish getting ready for her own workday. As she brushed her teeth, she noted the brightness in her eyes' reflection and the heightened color in her cheeks. Applying a touch of lipstick, she considered the outfit she was wearing with a smile of approval—a white skirt paired with a lettuce-green blouse that brought out the pale-green color of her eyes. She fluffed the waves of her short blond hair as Curtis thundered down the stairs.

"Grab some breakfast, honey," she called. "Mr. Kuzinsky said he'll feed you lunch, but you don't want to go there hungry."

Listening to him pour a bowl of cereal, she went to collect her laptop bag and purse, placing them both by the door and then peering out the window. He wouldn't make her late for work, would he?

Just then an older model, rust-colored Camry swung into the parking space in front of her house. Mr. Efficiency rolled up out of it, wearing a pair of triathlon sunglasses, khakis, and a gray T-shirt that highlighted his trim, muscular physique. His dark auburn hair matched the color of his car. He might be retired, but he moved like a young man, striding with purpose toward her door. She swung it open before he could knock.

"Good morning," she greeted him. *Goodness, was that breathy voice hers?*

He lowered the hand he'd lifted. "Am I late?"

"Of course not. Are you ever late?"

His eyes, crinkling at the corners, put a giddy feeling in her stomach. "Not usually," he admitted.

"Come on in," she said.

He didn't need to know that she'd cleaned her entire house yesterday in anticipation of his viewing it. Not a speck of dust dulled the shiny surfaces of her living room furniture.

"Nice space," he said taking in the open-concept lower level, with a kitchen leading to the stairs and master bedroom.

"Thanks. A rental, but it's kept up by the management." Shutting the door she caught the same scent she'd appreciated on Saturday—lemon and sage.

"Curtis is just finishing his breakfast." She nodded toward the breakfast bar where her son looked up from his cereal and stopped chewing.

Silence ensued as the two males assessed each other.

Rusty broke the spell. "Hello, Curtis," he said, crossing toward the breakfast bar and holding out a hand. "Name's Rusty. I knew your father," he added.

Curtis's eyes widened as they flicked in her direction. Oh, yeah. She'd forgotten to mention that part.

"You look a lot like him," Rusty added, releasing the boy's hand.

"That's what everyone says." Curtis finished

chewing and swallowed. "I don't remember him, though," he added without a trace of emotion.

A cloud seemed to descend over Rusty's head. He nodded and looked around the kitchen.

Maya found her hand on his solid shoulder.

He cast a sharp glance at her.

"I have to leave," she said with an apologetic grimace. "Do you mind locking up when you go?"

"I'm sure Curtis will handle that," he said, glancing at her son. "Have a good day at work, Maya. We'll be fine," he added.

But his tone was shot with the tiniest thread of uncertainty. And who could blame him? He'd never had kids. He had no idea what he was getting himself into.

"You can call me, you know, if you run into any trouble," she offered.

"No-o." He shook his head. "We'll be good," he said with more confidence.

She'd read once that SEALs used positive language to help construct positive outcomes. "Neuro-linguistic programming?" She cocked an eyebrow.

A short burst of laughter escaped him, wreathing his face with lines of pure amusement that made the breath tangle in her throat.

"Something like that," he admitted.

The urge to hug him overwhelmed her suddenly. Not only did she want to know if his body was as densely muscled as his shoulder suggested, but gratitude held her in a stranglehold. This arrangement sure beat leaving Curtis at loose ends with bad-news Santana hovering on the fringes and influencing her son in less-than-positive ways.

Reining herself in, she focused on Curtis. "Now, you listen to Mr. Kuzinsky and use your manners," she ordered.

"Yes, ma'am," Curtis said, though the sullenness in his gaze did not bode well in her opinion.

"I'll see you shortly after three," she added. "Bye, Rusty. Thanks again."

"No problem."

But there it was again—that reservation in his tone that suggested there might actually be a problem. Perhaps she just imagined it.

Hefting her bags, she let herself out of her condo and headed to her car, sidestepping a thirty-something man walking his Doberman Pinscher.

"Morning," she said, casting him a cautious smile as the dog swung its nose in her direction.

"How you doin'?" the man replied, sliding an oily gaze down the length of her body.

Maya stiffened. She had met this man some-where before—probably just out walking his dog. Something about him, either the grubby sweatpants or the thick gold necklace around his neck, warned her to keep her distance. Not for the first time did she consider moving to a safer neighborhood.

As he tugged the Doberman past her, she continued to her van, settled inside, and turned over the engine, cracking the windows to cool the warm interior. She was putting on her seatbelt and preparing to back out of her parking space when she saw the man stop and look back at her.

Given the expression on his face, he, too, was trying to recall how they knew each other. Maya sent him a forced smile then looked away in order to reverse her van. As she accelerated out of the condominium complex, a glance into her rearview mirror showed him standing in the same spot, ignoring his dog who tugged at the leash.

A *frisson* of alarm raised the downy hairs on Maya's forearms. Even across the ever-growing distance between them, she sensed the man's sudden hostility.

Time to move, she decided, picturing a quaint little house in the country and wondering what Rusty Kuzinsky's farmhouse looked like.

"OKAY, LISTEN UP," Rusty said, as he and Curtis rounded his house toward the crate he'd erected in the backyard the day before. He could hear the dog going crazy in it. He stopped walking, and the kid, who was already an inch taller than him, looked down and over at him.

Given the anxious look on Curtis's face, he didn't know the first thing about dogs. But that could be good, Rusty reasoned, because then maybe he had no preconceived notion that all dogs were sweet and loveable.

"Draco's not your average dog," he explained, though he'd already sketched Curtis a history of Draco's life—the extreme temperatures and hard work he'd endured and how many lives he'd saved. The kid already knew the dog was a hero. "You need to stand back a while and just watch me interact with him. Don't approach him until I introduce you. He's got some anxiety issues, which will go away eventually. But right now, he's still wired, you understand?"

Curtis nodded. Rusty thought he saw him swallow.

This was not the time to mention that the dog might bite if he wasn't careful. Christ, if the kid was any more fearful, Draco would smell his fear and run roughshod over him.

"We're going to walk around this corner, and you hang back about twenty feet while I let him out of the crate."

"Okay."

For all of his promising size, Curtis was obviously a cautious kid—not the type-A, my-nuts-are-bigger-than-my-brain type of young man that tried out for the Navy SEALs. But Rusty'd had his fill of young, intractable knuckleheads anyway. "Let's do this," he said.

Curtis trailed him to the corner of the house then stopped dead. Rusty couldn't blame him. Draco literally bounced off the walls of his crate. To say that he was going ballistic was an understatement. Rusty had left him penned a little too long. He'd have brought him along in the car, except that he'd seen Draco eat through the headrest of a Humvee once.

He called over his shoulder, raising his voice to be heard over the din, "He'll calm down in a minute."

Approaching the metal crate that shook with the force of Draco's lunges, he reached into the mailbox he'd mounted high on one side and withdrew a tennis ball. Standing over the dog, he summoned his dominant energy while holding the ball behind his back. "Draco, *zit*," he ordered, in the same commanding tone Nichols had used, and the dog snapped into a sitting position while quivering from his snout to the tip of his tail.

"You want this?" Rusty showed him the ball.

The dog quaked with the force of his prey drive, nostrils expanding and retracting with every breath. His once-liquid brown eyes still looked glassy and wild. Rusty heaved an inward sigh. He had his work cut out with this dog. Getting Maya's son involved might have been a huge mistake.

Feeling for the key in his pocket, he calmly unlocked the crate. He eased it out of the hole, pressing his weight against the door in case the dog lunged and pushed it open. "Draco, *blijf*," he ordered, gesturing for the dog to stay as he swung the door slowly open.

Draco didn't move a centimeter. His chest expanded and contracted like fireplace bellows.

Rusty backed slowly from the open door. "*Blijf*," he repeated. The dog watched, every muscle tensing like a coil about to spring free as he hurled the ball across the yard, nearly to the tree line.

He waited several seconds before speaking the word that sent the dog streaking out of the crate at the speed of light. "*Apport.*" Fetch.

Glancing back at Curtis, he found the kid's mouth hanging open. A glimmer of interest had replaced the wary look in his brown eyes.

For the next ten minutes, Rusty threw the ball while Draco retrieved it—again, again, and again, without any sign of the dog growing tired. At last, Rusty took the ball away, dropping it back into the mailbox and patting his thigh.

"*Hier,*" he said, signaling for the dog to flank him as he crossed back to where Curtis stood.

The kid visibly stiffened at their approach. The dog divided a gaze between the two humans, gauging Rusty's response to Curtis to determine whether he was friend or foe.

"Look at me," Rusty said, wresting Curtis's gaze upward. "Don't stare at the dog. Dogs communicate with body language, and staring means you want to fight."

Curtis glued wide eyes onto Rusty.

"You can look at him, just don't stare at him," Rusty amended. "Hold your hand out, palm side down, relaxing your fingers. Let him sniff you."

Curtis darted a fearful look at the dog. "He's not going to bite me, is he?"

Rusty longed to say, "Of course not," but then Draco might just make a liar out of him. "Just follow my directions and you'll be fine," he said, crossing his fingers mentally as Draco snuffled the boy's hand.

So far so good. "You can pet his head now."

The dog submitted to Curtis's tentative petting, but he didn't lean into the boy's hand the way he did to Rusty.

This wasn't going to be a case of love-at-first sight. Heaving an inward sigh, Rusty resolved to keep an eye on this pair all morning. His to-do list would simply have to wait, regardless of the fact that his guests were due in two days.

Curtis and Draco had forty-eight hours in which to bond.

"He likes you," Rusty lied. Draco's scorpion-curl tail indicated otherwise.

"I like his coloring," the kid admitted.

"He's darker than most Malinois. They tend to have more caramel with just a dark mask.

"Probably how he got his name," said the kid. "Draco's like Dracula."

"That's right." The comment proved the kid was a thinker. "Come on inside," he added. "You get to feed him breakfast."

CHAPTER FIVE

A WARM WELCOMING feeling enveloped Curtis as he followed the SEAL into the house's rear entry. "Wow," he exclaimed as he looked around the enormous kitchen.

"You like it?" the retired SEAL asked. He'd told Curtis to call him Rusty but Mr. Kuzinsky sounded more respectful. He wasn't going to get to know him well enough to call him Rusty, anyway.

"It's cool," Curtis said, embarrassed by his initial outburst.

The dog crossed straight to a set of bowls near the fireplace and lapped at his water.

Mr. Kuzinsky indicated the wooden bin next to the second bowl. "I keep his food in here. There's a scooper inside. Go ahead and put a scoop in his bowl, but first tell the dog to sit."

"*Zit*," Curtis said, mimicking the dog's master.

Draco ignored him.

"Say his name first and pair the command with this gesture." Mr. Kuzinsky swept up a closed fist in what looked like an upper punch.

Curtis copied him. "Draco, *zit.*"

The dog stopped drinking and looked up at him. Thoughts seemed to shift behind his keen gaze as he slowly sank onto his haunches.

"*Braaf,*" Mr. Kuzinsky praised him. "That means good. Now go ahead and put a scoop into his bowl."

Curtis felt the dog's hot breath flow across his forearm as he bent over and scooped out the required amount of food. *Please don't bite me,* he thought dumping it into the bowl and straightening quickly.

Without waiting for a release, the dog lunged for the bowl and started scarfing up his breakfast.

Mr. Kuzinsky clicked his tongue in disapproval.

Listening to Draco pulverize the kibble between his powerful jaws, Curtis's stomach knotted when the man said, "Now take the bowl away from him."

"But he's not done."

"I know. But we need to teach him that good things come from you."

Regarding the dog's dark head buried in his bowl, Curtis swallowed. "I don't think I should."

"Try it."

The softly spoken suggestion left no option to defy.

With an indrawn breath, Curtis sank into a cautious crouch and reached slowly for the bowl, intending to ease it away. A menacing growl rumbled in the dog's chest and he snatched his hand back.

To his surprise, the former SEAL grabbed the back of his T-shirt at the same time and hauled him to his feet. "Maybe next time," he said, moving surreptitiously between him and the dog.

And that's when it dawned on Curtis that the animal was dangerous, and this man knew it. What the hell had his mother gotten him into? Did she want him out of the house so bad that she didn't even care about his safety?

"You hungry?" Mr. Kuzinsky asked, acting like nothing had happened. "Want anything to drink?"

Curtis shook his head. Dismay put a knot in his throat so that he couldn't speak.

"Let's take the dog for a walk. I'll show you around, and Draco can get used to you."

Curtis remained silent and the man raised his eyebrows at him. "Okay?" he prompted.

"Yes, sir," Curtis said through a tight throat.

"Rusty," the man reminded him.

Curtis nodded, but his tongue refused to form the name.

CUED BY THE GPS on her phone, Maya turned at the nondescript mailbox onto a long pebbled driveway off Muddy Creek Road. A stand of centuries-old oak trees blocked the view of the house coming up on her left, though she could make out a shiny tin roof, suggesting a structure of impressive proportions. As she passed the trees, the house came abruptly into view.

Holy smokes. While the word quaint hovered at the periphery of her mind, the house was just too large for that description. Architectural details like whitewashed clapboard siding and a covered veranda dated its original construction to the turn of the twentieth century. But given the HVAC unit half-hidden behind a hedge of young boxwoods, it had clearly been renovated and updated.

The oak trees in the front yard cast shade over the front veranda while the hot June sun glanced off the tin roof at the back. Acres of land stretched in every direction to include a pinewood forest and marshlands which, according to her GPS concealed a creek that went clear out to the sound. What a spread!

Recognizing Rusty's car, she slowed to a stop alongside it while hunting for any sign of Curtis and the dog he was supposed to be caring for.

Her heart pattered at the expectation of spending a few minutes with Rusty Kuzinsky. As she closed the car door behind her, a strident bark shattered the still, warm silence. Following the sound to the rear of the house, she halted abruptly at the sight of the dog trotting in her direction, unrestrained in any way. As their eyes met, he planted his feet and bristled, tail arching over his back like a stinger. She hardly dared to breathe.

"Draco." Curtis stood some distance behind him holding a tennis ball. "*Apport*," he called, and the dog glanced back just as Curtis hurled the ball in the opposite direction.

Draco wheeled away, streaking after it, and Maya released the breath she was holding.

In the same instant, Rusty stepped out of his back door and her heart continued thumping for a completely different reason.

"He makes a good watch dog," she commented, subtly drying her sweaty palms on her white skirt.

"Yes, he does." He spared a glance for the dog, that had caught up to his prize at the edge of the trees and was headed back toward them. "You found the place okay?"

"GPS," she said. "I thought you'd at least have a sign up by the mailbox. Bronco said you named this place Never Forget?"

"Yes, but anonymity is safer." His dark eyes drifted over her as he came nearer—too quickly to construe as flirtatious, but there was no mistaking the appreciative gleam in his dark irises.

"Right. You wouldn't want to draw attention to yourselves." Out of the corner of her eye, she saw the dog deliver the ball to Curtis. "So, how'd it go?" she asked, forcing herself to watch her son's exchange with the dog when every cell in her body was fixated on Rusty.

"Not bad," he replied, with just enough reservation to raise a red flag.

She looked sharply over at him. "Why? What happened?"

"Watch," he invited, nodding at the boy and dog.

With a word Maya didn't recognize, Curtis ordered the dog to drop the ball, but the dog held onto his prize. Dancing around Curtis, he shook his head as if whipping an animal around between his jaws to snap its neck.

Curtis put his hands on his hips and drew himself to his full height.

"That's it," Rusty called, letting her know this was something he'd taught her son to do.

"*Los*," Curtis repeated in a firm voice.

The dog ignored him for several more seconds, then tossed his head and released the ball at the same time, lobbing it toward him.

"*Braaf*," Curtis said, scooping it up. Instead of throwing it again, he marched over to what had to be the dog's crate and dropped the ball into a container mounted on the side.

Draco pursued him, releasing a rash of angry barks. Curtis visibly cringed as if expecting to be bitten.

Rusty strode in their direction. "*Foei!*" he shouted at the dog, which stopped his barking and backed off.

With a look of profound relief, Curtis hurried in Maya's direction. "Are we going home now?"

She hadn't wanted to leave just yet. In fact, she longed to go inside and see the restorations Bronco had told her about. This farmhouse had been virtually uninhabitable when Rusty purchased it a year ago.

"Curtis has worked hard," he stated turning back. A crease of what might have been worry furrowed his forehead. "Why don't you call me later?"

Maya had transferred his number from the business card into her cellphone contacts. "Sure." It was clear he wanted to discuss Curtis's first day without her son overhearing. That had to mean something bad had happened. Her hopes for a semi-permanent arrangement floundered.

"Say good-bye to Rusty," she prompted as Curtis turned away.

"Bye," he said over his shoulder.

With Curtis out of sight, Rusty approached her

quickly, and her pulse quickened. She wished she hadn't wilted instantly in the heat, her blouse sticking to the light film of sweat that dampened her bra.

"Here's the money he earned today," he said, pulling out his wallet and extracting several bills.

She glanced down at the small wad he held out to her. "That's way too much money."

"It'll get him to come back tomorrow."

She hesitated at the telling statement then took the money. "That bad?" she asked.

Their fingertips touched in the tradeoff, affecting her like a warm brush of lips.

"It'll get better," he promised.

"I'll call tonight," she replied.

"Good."

They regarded each other another moment longer before Maya turned away, crossing the lawn on spongy knees. She slipped into her hot van next to a scowling Curtis, started it up, and cranked the A/C.

"I'm not coming here tomorrow," he insisted as she put the vehicle in reverse.

Disappointment ambushed her. She guarded her response until she finished turning the van around and was starting down the long driveway. "What makes you say that?" she asked.

"That dog is insane. He almost bit me like four times."

She glanced over at him, somewhat alarmed to

hear it but hoping Curtis was exaggerating. "I don't see any bite marks," she observed.

"Only because Mr. Kuzinsky called him off every time."

"He's watching out for you then." Relief edged her worry aside. "He's not going to let you get bitten."

"Hah. I'm not going back." Turning his head, he stared mulishly out the passenger's side window. "I hate that dog."

Maya handed him the money she held between her palm and the steering wheel. "Here's your pay," she said breezily.

Glimpsing his surprise as he took the bills, she hoped there'd be no more talk of not returning.

"You need to save that," she added as Curtis leaned forward so he could shove the bills into the back pocket of his shorts. "In two years, you'll have your driver's license. What do you think you're going to drive?"

"Not this ugly thing," he asserted.

"Correct." She cast him a sugar-coated smile.

He retreated into silence as they flew up the boulevard headed toward their neighborhood. She could only assume Curtis was weighing the pros and cons of keeping his job.

"By the end of summer, I could save five hundred dollars," he mused out loud.

Victory. A warm tide spread through her. She would get to see Rusty again. It was a shame he was emptying his pockets just to help her out, however. Maybe there was something she could do for him in exchange?

"All right, I'll go back," Curtis conceded suddenly, "on one condition."

"Oh?" What made him think he held the upper hand?

"You take away my grounding. It isn't fair that I have to work all day and then I can't hang out with friends afterward."

He had a point there. Nor did she particularly want him underfoot at the end of her day.

"How about a compromise?" she countered. "You may hang out with your friends from four to seven, but you're home after that."

He made a sound of disgust and rolled his eyes. "Fine," he said.

"But no hanging out with Santana."

"Why not?" The face he turned on her was the very picture of affront.

"He's trouble, that's why."

"Oh, come on."

"You come on. He's at least sixteen, and he's extremely rude."

"He's in my grade," Curtis retorted. "Are you racist or something?"

"What?" She pictured Santana's swarthy skin and

realized for the first time that he was of mixed race. "Of course not. Race has nothing to do with it."

"Sure it doesn't."

"Wow. You know what?" She caught herself back from recanting on her decision to let him off of his grounding. Did she really want a rebellious, angry teenager wrecking her peaceful evenings? No. She would try another tactic. "I trust your judgment, Curtis. If Santana tries to influence you in any bad way—if he offers you drugs or makes you watch porn or something—"

"Mom!" He affected a look of disgust.

"—then I trust you to walk away, understand? I raised you to be respectful of your elders, to think about your future, and to stay clear of trouble. Now I expect you to monitor yourself on all those fronts. You're practically an adult."

"Okaaay." He drawled out the word as if waiting for the other shoe to fall. "So I can hang out with him?"

She cringed at the mere thought. "As long as his behaviors don't rub off on you." *Any more than they have already,* she added silently.

"They won't," he promised, making her feel a little hopeful. "Thanks," he added, sending her a remnant of his little boy smile, the one full of love for his mother.

How she missed those simpler days.

CHAPTER SIX

CURTIS BACKED AWAY from Santana's front door after knocking. It sounded like Draco was inside the house, barking furiously and clawing the door, but Santana didn't even own a dog.

Puzzled, Curtis checked the house number, making sure he was in the right place. The door swung open, and a Doberman Pinscher strained through the opening, caught back by a dark-skinned stranger, who held the growling menace by his studded leather collar.

Curtis tore his nervous gaze off the dog's snarling visage. "Uh, is Santana home?"

The man regarded him with hard eyes. "He just left for Walmart with his mom."

"Oh." Noticing a family resemblance, Curtis guessed that the stranger was a relative.

"You want to wait inside?"

Considering the stranger's hostile look, the offer

caught Curtis by surprise.

"Santana won't be long," the man added.

The dog continued to snarl.

"Shut up, Lucifer," the man scolded.

"No, that's all right," Curtis said, thinking the dog's name suited him. "I'll wait until I see his mom's car."

Hard eyes drifted over him again. "You're that special investigator's son," the relative stated. "Schultz, right?"

Curtis nodded. "Yeah, you know my mom?"

"We've met," he said. "I'm Santana's Uncle Will," he said.

Curtis nodded and backed off the stoop. "Nice to meet you, Mr. Will. I'll come back later."

"You do that," said Will, managing a smile that failed to reach his eyes.

As he walked away, Curtis could feel the man watching him. It was pretty obvious Santana's uncle didn't like his mom. She'd told him before that a lot of the men she worked with didn't like her. Men had issues with women who were as tough as they were. He probably shouldn't mention Santana's uncle—or his dog—to his mom.

RUSTY FORCED HIMSELF to let his cellphone ring three times before he cleared his throat and answered it. "Kuzinsky," he said out of habit.

"Hi, it's Maya."

Her voice sounded huskier on the phone. He pictured her lying back on her bed, the shoes kicked off her tiny feet, her purple-framed spectacles on a nearby nightstand next to a glass of red wine. The PG-rated vision aroused him instantly. How pathetic was that?

"Well, you don't sound like you're mad at me, so that's good," he began.

"Why would I be mad at you?" Her tone dismissed the mere idea.

"For putting your son in harm's way?" he suggested.

She hummed her acknowledgment. "He did say that the dog is crazy."

"Yeah, well..." He couldn't deny it. "War does that to everyone."

Her sudden silence made him want to retract the depressing statement.

"I know it does," she said, with enough compassion to reassure him. "But I trust you to know the difference between crazy and dangerous. You watched over Curtis today. Just promise me you'll remain that vigilant until the dog settles down."

His hopes rose. "Does that mean he's coming back tomorrow?"

"Yes. Absolutely."

He closed his eyes briefly. "Good. It was touch and go today," he admitted. "Draco could sense Curtis's fear. Your son needs to establish himself as the alpha, which could take time and can't really be taught."

"I'm sorry," she apologized. "I know you have better things to do than babysit my son."

"It's not a problem." Except that it sort of was a problem. His SEALs were showing up tomorrow evening.

"There are so many pitfalls awaiting teens these days. I see corrupting influences everywhere, and there's only so much I can do to protect him when I work every day. So, thank you. I'm really grateful for this distraction."

"Don't thank me yet," he begged. "We've got a long way to go."

"I will understand if it becomes too much," she said.

An unmistakable warmth emanated from the vicinity of his heart. Hearing Maya's gratitude, he didn't care how hard it got. "We'll play it by ear," he promised.

"Is there ... anything that I can do to return the favor?"

The ideas that popped into his head weren't suitable to mention. In fact, they tied his tongue in knots, keeping him from saying anything.

"What about your list?" she suggested.

"My list?"

"You know. The shopping list you had at Home Depot. Did you find everything on it?"

"Uh, not yet." But he wasn't about to ask her to go shopping for him.

"What do you still need?"

The opportunity dropped so suddenly into his lap, he couldn't afford to let it pass. "A date," he suggested.

"A date?"

Her startled tone had him backpedaling.

"Well, I'm taking Friday night to myself to get away from the house and all the guys who'll be here. I thought I'd make a small bonfire on the beach, but if you'd rather not…" Maybe she wasn't interested. Maybe he'd completely misread her.

"No, that sounds nice," she said with slightly more enthusiasm, yet still a hint of reservation. "It's just … I haven't been on a date in over a decade."

Suddenly, there was Ian Schultz's ghost standing right in front him, just looking at him.

Rusty gripped his phone harder. "Look, if it makes you uncomfortable, I'll be okay by myself."

"No, I'd like to join you," she stated haltingly.

"You sure?" he asked. She didn't sound sure.

"Yeah, I think so."

Maybe she just needed time to adjust to the idea.

"In the meantime," she added skirting the subject suddenly, "let's see how Curtis does on his second day."

Ah, so a date with him depended on what happened between the boy and the dog.

"Fair enough," he replied. After all, the dog could end up biting the kid. The mother could end up blaming *him*. All hopes for a romance might burn completely to the ground. But hope was a stubborn son-of-a-gun, and he was still going to try. "I'll see you in the morning," he said.

"Yeah. I'll see you."

At least he could tell that she was smiling when he hung up.

Rusty shoved his phone back into his pocket and returned Ian Schultz's steady regard. He suffered an urge to stick his tongue out at the man.

"She must have really loved you," he said to the big, burly warrior.

Sometimes the ghosts talked back to him; sometimes they ignored him. Ian just shrugged with macho confidence.

"You got a problem with me asking her out?" Rusty asked.

Sliding his hands into the pockets of his desert camouflage BDUs, Ian looked Rusty over as if measuring up the competition. At long last, he shook his head.

67

"What's that mean? You don't mind, or you think I can't win her over?"

The ghost sent him a knowing smile. And then he vanished just as suddenly as he'd appeared.

Rusty sank onto the edge of his bed and scrubbed a hand over his face. What would a woman who based her career on facts and hard evidence say to his assertion that he saw dead people—including her late husband?

She'd accepted his offer of a date with lukewarm enthusiasm for a reason. Maybe he just didn't live up to the standards she was used to.

The sound of jets buzzing his rooftop on their descent to Oceana Naval Air Station prompted Draco to fly into a panic. Crated out back, his strident barks resonated with irrational fear.

Poor dog. Poor him.

Rusty heaved a tired sigh. His SEALs would show up tomorrow and he hadn't put so much as a dent in his to-do list since the dog showed up. Maybe he ought to take up Maya's offer of help after all.

CHAPTER SEVEN

"CAN YOU GET the door, honey?" Maya called to Curtis.

Rusty's offer of a date for the weekend had led to a fitful night's sleep. Her alarm had failed to awaken her on time, and now she was frantically applying makeup so as not to be late for the meeting with a JAG officer regarding three airmen who'd managed to steal weapons from Logistics, probably to sell on the black market. With scanty evidence to prosecute them, Maya feared the men were going to get away with their trafficking.

Curtis crossed the living room, his footsteps audible through her bathroom wall. She heard him open the door, heard Rusty greet him.

Just the sound of Rusty's voice put a tremor in her fingers. All of this angst for what? It wasn't like he'd asked her to marry him! She blinked at the startling thought, smudging her mascara. She reached for a tissue to wipe it off.

A bonfire on the beach was a harmless proposition. But fires and beaches were so darned romantic. A couple couldn't walk beside the waves without holding hands. They couldn't sit in the glow of a snapping fire and not feel a kindling of desire. It had been so long since she'd done either, she feared she'd make a fool of herself.

What were Rusty's intentions, anyway? He'd been a bachelor all his life. Was he thinking of settling down and starting a family? She'd already done that—had no wish to do it again.

But starting a family would compete with Never Forget Retreat. Perhaps he was only looking for a good time. A little fun, a light romance.

She had never done "light romance" or one-night stands—ever. She and Ian had met at Texas A&M. They'd been each other's firsts. She could scarcely remember the rituals involved in dating.

With Rusty she wanted more than a dalliance. Until she knew what his agenda was, her only course of action was to hold back.

Casting a harried glance at the peach shell and black skirt she wore, she squared her shoulders and exited her bedroom, running straight into Rusty, who stood at the breakfast bar in her kitchen. Curtis was wolfing down his cereal. Rusty waited, tapping an index card on the granite counter top.

He turned at her approach, and her nerves started jangling all over again.

"Hi," she said, moving to stand beside her son.

"Good morning." Rusty's haggard aspect suggested he hadn't slept well either. Why not? Had he expected her to leap at his proposition?

"What's that?" she asked, glancing at the card.

He tapped it two more times then held it out to her to take. "You asked if I'd found everything on my list. I'm still looking for these items."

Pleased that he'd taken her up on her offer, she took the card and skimmed it. Only five items comprised the list which included an off-white trash bin for a bathroom and a dog brush.

"I'll take care of this," she promised. The offer made her feel better about stringing him along. "In fact, I'll have them for you by this afternoon when I come to collect Curtis."

"That'd be great," he said, his manner subdued. "Good luck finding the trash can, though. I've looked everywhere for a metal one."

"I'll find it," she promised.

Curtis swung off of his stool and carried his bowl to the sink.

"Teeth," Maya said as he started for the front door.

Rolling his eyes at her, he turned back to do her bidding.

"Kids." Maya heaved an exaggerated sigh and shook her head.

Rusty just stood there looking at her.

"Are you worried about your guests coming tomorrow?" she fished.

He grimaced and nodded. "Yeah."

"How many will you have?"

"A whole platoon. Sixteen men."

"That many? How on earth are you going to feed them all?"

"I have cooks coming in."

"Really! Who's—I'm sorry, I'm totally prying here—but where does the money come from to feed them?" She stepped closer, interested in his answer.

"Various sources. I won a couple of grants, and I have private donors, mostly former SEALs who see the benefit of what I'm trying to do."

"You do all of the bookkeeping, too?"

"The bookkeeping, the shopping, contracting with people to come in and offer various types of therapy."

"There's so much to it," she marveled. "You must be exhausted."

He sent her a weary smile. "Do I look exhausted?"

"Kind of," she said with sympathy and a wry smile. The offer to help him out further trembled on the tip of her tongue, but with Curtis thundering down the stairs, the time wasn't right.

"Time to roll," Rusty said to her son.

Maya's heart stopped and then started again. That was what Ian used to say!

"See you this afternoon," Rusty called as he and Curtis headed toward the door.

Watching them leave, Maya was struck by her desire to lend a hand. Rusty truly seemed overwhelmed. Taking on a traumatized dog on top of everything else had to be wearing him down. And now he had her teenager to look after, as well.

Glancing at the list he'd given her, she vowed to find everything on it. Then maybe he'd let her help in other ways.

Ten minutes later, she locked up her condo and made her way to her van. She'd forgotten about the man with the Doberman until she saw him in her side view mirror standing on the opposite sidewalk, watching her departure.

The same sense of recognition niggled, and suddenly she remembered who he was—one of the three sailors facing charges for stealing a weapons shipment. What a coincidence! She would be working on his case that morning, trying to find evidence that still eluded her. Two crates of rifles couldn't simply disappear into thin air.

No wonder the man was glaring at her. What was his name again? She combed her memory. Ah yes, Petty Officer 2nd Class William Goddard. Pending his hearing, he'd been relieved of active duty, a quarter of his pay docked since he wasn't working.

And he lived in her neighborhood? Yikes. She was going to have to invest in an alarm system or, better yet, move before NCIS found him guilty and vengeful thoughts filled his head.

She did have something to be grateful for—at least Curtis wasn't home by himself anymore. Thank goodness for Rusty Kuzinsky.

"WHATCHA GOT THERE, dog?"

Curtis transferred his gaze from the sparkling water of the creek to the muddy shore where Draco barked at something he'd come across. In the still silence of the great outdoors, the only other sound was the rustling of marsh grass and the keening cry of the osprey circling overhead.

Heaving himself off the dock, Curtis went to investigate. He'd put Draco on the thirty-foot lead, winding most of it around one of the pier's pilings while leaving just enough slack for the dog to entertain himself.

Apparently, Draco had found something of interest. His hackles bristled and his tail arched over his back the same way it did when Curtis showed him the ball. The dog bowed low, stretching out his front legs, barked, and then pounced, only to back away and bow again.

Coming up behind him, Curtis caught sight of a large Virginia blue crab cornered against a rotting log. It stood its ground, defending itself with outstretched pincers. Curtis knew from experience how painful those pincers could be.

"*Foei!*" he said to the dog, telling him no.

But Draco ignored him, continuing to lunge toward the crab and then dodge out of its reach, teasing the crab into going on the offensive.

Picturing the crab grabbing hold of Draco's sensitive nose, Curtis took up the leash and pulled the dog away from the threat. "*Foei,*" he said again. "*Los,*" he added, using the words Rusty had taught him, though the dog couldn't release something he hadn't grabbed yet.

As he pulled Draco back, he kicked his sneakered foot at the crab, intending to punt it over the log and into the marsh where it could hide.

What happened next occurred so fast he hardly saw it, just the dog's head moving forward at the same time as his foot. Shock kept him from crying out as he snatched his leg back and looked down. There was no denying what had happened. Blood welled from three visible puncture wounds just above his sock.

The flipping dog had bitten him!

Unconcerned with the damage he'd wrought, Draco lunged for his prize a second time. Without Curtis's leg in the way, he seized the crab with one bite. *Crunch.* The crab was dead before it could pinch him. Draco looked up at him expectantly, the crustacean dangling from his mouth.

"You bit me, you sonofabitch!" Curtis shouted.

The dog flinched from him, clearly startled by the outburst.

The numbness that accompanied Curtis's shock gave way to sudden pain. "Shit!" he added. Lifting his head to look back at the house, he hunted for Mr. Kuzinsky, who'd gone inside citing the need to make phone calls.

No one was coming to his rescue. He'd have to get to the house by himself.

Hopping on one foot, he started up the bank before remembering the dog. He'd been told not to leave the dog alone with the lead or Draco would chew through it. Fine.

Unfurling the length of nylon off the piling, Curtis started to limp toward the house with the dog following behind, dead crab still in his mouth.

Halfway to his destination, it occurred to him that Mr. Kuzinsky had told him not to take anything away from the dog unless he was around to monitor the situation. He hadn't thought of kicking the crab as taking it away, but it really was one and the same. So, theoretically, it was his fault the dog had bitten him.

Glancing back at Draco as he limped the rest of the way to the house, Curtis also realized the dog had been in little danger of getting pinched by the blue crab. Those formidable pincers now dangled limply out of either side of the dog's mouth.

The dog's earnest gaze locked on him. Was it his imagination or did Draco's chocolaty eyes hold a hint of remorse?

Curtis led him straight to his crate. "In," he said, not knowing the Dutch command. Draco padded resolutely inside, laid the dead crab in one corner, then sat in front of it to guard it, while Curtis locked the door.

With his hands still on the crate, Curtis looked down at his ankle. Blood pulsed from the puncture wounds. As he pulled his sock higher to cover the holes and slow the bleeding, it occurred to him that what had happened was a game changer. His mom was going to freak out. She wouldn't let him come here anymore, which meant that he'd have nothing to do for the rest of the summer and he wouldn't be making any money.

Self-pity overwhelmed him suddenly. His ankle hurt too much to put any weight on it. So he sat right there on the grass next to Draco's crate, stuck his bad leg out, rested his head on the knee of his good leg and let the tears spring to his eyes.

A soft whining sound had him looking over his shoulder. Draco had approached as close as he could get with the bars of the crate between them. Looking as woeful as Curtis felt, the dog hung his head and whined again.

"Now you're sorry?" Gazing at the dog's despondent demeanor, Curtis was certain that he was.

Heck, if that crab had been an enemy combatant, then Draco had done the job he was trained to do and eliminated the threat.

"It's not your fault," he realized. As the ramifications occurred to him a second time, he shook off his self-pity and struggled to his feet. If he wanted to come back here—and he did—he would need to convince first Mr. Kuzinsky and then his mom that the dog was blameless.

RUSTY WAS JUST heading to the kitchen to cast an eye at the marsh when Curtis pushed his way inside, visibly limping.

His gaze dropped to the kid's blood-soaked sock, and he knew without even seeing the puncture wounds that Draco had bit him. "Son of a bitch," he muttered, before recalling the need to temper his language.

"It wasn't his fault." The kid's voice cracked. He

fought to keep from crying. "He thought I was taking a crab from him, but I was just trying to keep it from pinching him."

In his mind's eye, Rusty had a clear picture of the way it had gone down.

"Sit," he ordered, sliding one of the chairs from the farm table behind Curtis's knees. "Let's see how bad it is," he added, tackling Curtis's tennis shoe before the boy had fully sat down. He pulled it off as gently as he could, engendering a hiss of pain. Peeling the sock just over Curtis's heel, he took in the three deep puncture wounds with mounting dismay.

His hopes for a date on the beach with Maya went up in a cloud of smoke.

Damn it. He should have seen this coming. To be honest, he *had* seen it coming but he'd been so blinded by his desire to pull Maya closer that he'd disregarded the risk to her son. And like any proper mother, she had every right to defend her cub, forbidding Curtis to care for the dog from here on. Rusty would be lucky if she even spoke to him again. He hoped to God he wasn't looking at a lawsuit.

"It's not too bad." He spoke the words any wounded man wanted to hear.

"Don't tell my mom, or she won't let me come back here."

The kid's concerns mirrored his own. "I hear

you, but you can't hide this from her. Let's clean you up first so it doesn't get infected."

"We don't have to tell her," the boy continued with surprising insistence. "Please, I want to come back. It wasn't Draco's fault. He was doing what he'd been trained to do."

It was the sheen of tears in Curtis's eyes that caused Rusty to waver. They could, perhaps, get away with cleaning the wound really well and then hiding it with a fresh pair of socks. She might be none the wiser.

"I don't know, son. You're mom's a smart woman. She's bound to find out." He realized he'd be a fool to try and deceive her.

"Well, don't call her yet," Curtis pleaded. "She has an important case this morning. She's too busy to get away." He wiped an errant tear away with the ball of his fist.

Rusty had to respect the boy's wishes. "Okay," he agreed. "Let me get my first aid kit. Let's let it bleed a while. It's washing out any bacteria that might have been on Draco's teeth. Be right back."

"We can't take too long," Curtis called after him. "Draco hasn't had his run yet."

CHAPTER EIGHT

MAYA DROVE UP the driveway, proud of the fact that she'd found everything on Rusty's wish list. He'd been right about the small metal waste bin. It had been the hardest thing to find, but she'd found the perfect one in the last store she'd visited. By bringing it to him, might she be offered a tour of the majestic farmhouse?

Parking in the same spot as yesterday, she gathered her purchases off the back seat and carried them to the back of the house. There she found Curtis lobbing the ball to the dog, who scarcely glanced in her direction before focusing on the ball.

"Hey, Mom," Curtis sang out.

Wondering at his overly cheerful tone, Maya transferred her gaze to the outdoor picnic table where Rusty sat with a pile of paperwork before him and a tall glass of water beside that. At her approach, he put his pen down and looked up. One look at his taut expression and she knew something had happened. She couldn't help her step from faltering for a moment before she reached the table and plunked down all her hard sought treasures.

"Is everything okay?" She wished she didn't sound like such an anxious mom, but she'd lived through the worst and knew it could happen.

The crease on his forehead deepened, and his lips firmed into a straight line. "Curtis has something to tell you," he said, waving her son over.

Calling the dog, Curtis started in their direction. Seeing his slight limp, Maya feared the worst, but she could see no sign of injury. Curtis ordered the dog to sit and stay. Draco obeyed him. With his tongue lolling out one side of his mouth, he stared at Curtis, awaiting more commands. They'd come a long way from yesterday.

"What do you want to tell me?" Maya prompted.

"Well…" Curtis glanced at Rusty, who nodded his encouragement. "Draco was messing with a crab down at the pier." He pointed toward the marsh. "I thought the crab was going to pinch his nose so I tried kicking it out of the way. Draco thought I was taking it from him, and he kind of bit me on the ankle."

Her worried gaze dropped to his ankle which was hidden by a sock too white to be his own.

"How bad is it?" she asked, glancing again at

Rusty's grim expression.

"Not too bad," Curtis said.

"Superficial," Rusty echoed.

"Can you show me?" she requested.

Curtis bent over and peeled the sock away from his skin. She spotted at least two puncture wounds surrounded by red and slightly swollen flesh.

"I followed protocol for animal bites and cleaned it out with warm soap and water," Rusty added. "Only thing to do now is to keep it clean and dry. If it starts to show signs of infection, a topical oint-ment ought to be enough."

Maya didn't know what to say. Dismay held a tight grip on her vocal cords.

"It's my fault," Curtis insisted. "Rusty told me not to take anything away from Draco unless he was there."

"And I was making phone calls," Rusty inserted. "I'm sorry. I should have been keeping a closer eye on them."

She shook her head. "Don't apologize for that," she said. "You have your own work to do. Maybe this wasn't the best idea," she heard herself say.

Curtis made a sound of disgust. "I told you we shouldn't have told her," he said to Rusty.

Realizing they'd discussed keeping her in the dark about the incident, her anger flared without warning.

"Of course you had to tell me," she said, staring hard at her son. Then she turned to Rusty. "How do we know the dog won't bite him in the face next time or on the hand?" she asked him.

"He won't bite me again," Curtis insisted.

"I didn't ask you, honey. I asked Mr. Kuzinsky."

Rusty just looked at her, his dark eyes troubled. "Why don't you call me later and we'll talk about it," he suggested quietly.

His mature and reasonable reply made her feel childish.

"Of course," she agreed. But she was pretty sure he wouldn't have the words to reassure her that her son was perfectly safe. Clearly the dog was more dangerous than he'd believed, or he would never have brought in a teenage boy to play with it in the first place—right?

Recalling her purchases, she gestured to the bags now splayed across the picnic table. "Here's all the stuff on your list. I found the trash bin," she added, pulling it out of the bag to show off her accomplishment in finding it. "Is this about right?"

He mustered a smile for her. "Yes, it's perfect. Thank you." There was so much formality in his tone that her heart fell. As far as he was concerned, Curtis wouldn't be coming back, which meant their potential date this weekend was probably on the chopping block, as well.

"Well, I'd better get Curtis home," she said.

Curtis divided a puzzled gaze between the two adults but held his tongue.

Rusty reached into his back pocket and pulled out several bills and handed them to Curtis. "Here you go, son. Thanks for your help."

"You're welcome."

Maya bit her tongue against the same protest as the day before. It seemed like too much for just watching a dog, but, in this case, Curtis had earned that money today—and then some.

"I'll call you," she promised, heading toward her car.

There was no giddy feeling in her stomach like there'd been twenty-four hours earlier. As far as she could tell, Rusty considered their arrangement over. At the corner of the house, she glanced back to see him squatting beside the dog, petting him absently and staring out into the marsh. Draco gave a whine as Curtis turned the corner.

What was *he* sad about? The damn dog had ruined everything.

As SHE'D DONE the previous evening, Maya dialed Rusty's number at quarter to eight. A queasy feeling usurped the anticipation she'd felt when calling him the night before. She sat on her bed, glancing briefly up at Ian's portrait, before looking away.

Surely Rusty understood that her first priority was her son's welfare. And recalling the finality in his voice that day, he had probably already guessed she would want to keep Curtis away from Draco from now on. After all, what guarantee could he give that the dog wouldn't bite Curtis again? And next time the ramifications could be worse. A bite to the face could leave her son permanently disfigured.

On the other hand, without the dog to watch, Curtis would be home alone, with a potential arms smuggler watching her house and brooding over the possibility that he might soon go to jail.

More than that, an end to Curtis's dog-sitting translated to an end to any potential romance between her and Rusty. She'd like to unlink the two entirely so that she didn't end up putting Curtis at risk just to satisfy her desire to get to know Rusty better. But if she *did* unlink them, then the bonfire on the beach might never transpire, and she was looking forward to it—more than she wanted to admit.

Without an excuse to visit Rusty's farmhouse and with their lives so busy, they'd never see each other again. She'd continue her solitary existence indefinitely.

Until last autumn, that option had been fine with her. Meeting Rusty for the first time had awakened her dormant spirit. Suddenly, ten years of solitude struck her as an awfully long time to be alone. Here she was, still in her thirties. Why shouldn't she get another shot at forever?

If she only knew Rusty's intentions. Given all the distractions with the dog and the upcoming arrival of his visitors, he might prefer to stay single and unencumbered.

His phone rang and rang, suggesting that was probably the case. Or maybe he just wished to avoid a less-than-pleasant conversation. Unprepared to leave a message—so much depended on his responses—she hung up, opting to try again later.

Leaving the phone on her dresser, she went to check on Curtis.

To her surprise, he wasn't toggling a controller in an attempt to obliterate space aliens or enemy combatants. Instead, he was sitting at his desk, reading off a website. The photos on the page told her he was researching dogs of the same breed as Draco.

"What are you doing?" she asked, coming to stand behind him.

"These Belgian Malinois are amazing dogs," he said with zeal. "They're the most fearless dogs in the world, bred for protection for centuries as protectors. They'll even jump out of airplanes at high altitudes wearing an oxygen mask. How cool is that?"

"Are you serious?"

"Yep. Right here, see?" He showed her a picture of a dog like Draco wearing a harness and a face mask, fur flying as he plummeted through the air in the arms of an operative with a parachute.

"They're like secret weapons, these dogs. Terrorists are deathly afraid of them." He read her a paragraph brimming with accounts of lives saved as dogs detected hidden explosives and ammunition caches. "Draco must be bored out of his mind after doing all this stuff."

Hearing the pride and awe in Curtis's voice, Maya felt her concerns give way to a different feeling. Something like gratitude uplifted her. Suddenly her son, whose life had revolved around the latest PS4 release, was interested in a real-world phenomenon—keeping operatives safe from terrorists. In just two days, and despite having been bitten, Curtis was all about this crazy dog.

"You really don't think Draco will bite you again?" she asked, revealing her main concern.

He craned his neck to look up at her. "I know he won't," he said with conviction. "He knew the minute it happened what he did. I saw it in his eyes. Please, Mom, I want to go back. And it's not about the money either. That dog needs me right now."

His words rocked her back on her heels. The

dog needed Curtis, and Curtis needed the dog. She ought to give them both another chance. But what about Rusty, who hadn't answered her phone call? His tone earlier that day had suggested his realization that the liabilities involved weren't worth his time or his money.

"Can I go back tomorrow?" Curtis pressed.

"I don't know, honey. I haven't gotten through to Rusty yet."

"Well, try again."

She ruffled his hair. "All right. I'll try again."

Curtis went back to his monitor. "Let me know what he says," he called as she walked away.

Returning to her bedroom downstairs, Maya picked up her phone to see if Rusty had called her back. He hadn't. Heaving an uncertain sigh, she thought for a moment about what she should say, then she dialed his number, ready to leave a message this time.

AT SHORTLY AFTER midnight, Rusty collapsed onto his bed with barely enough energy to crawl beneath the sheets. He patted the comforter, summoning the dog up next to him.

With Draco turning circles between his legs, Rusty suddenly remembered Maya was supposed to call him earlier that evening. Concern that he'd missed her call had him swiping his cellphone off its charger to check.

"Damn it."

Sure enough, she'd called him—twice. He'd been too busy welcoming his guests to Never Forget Retreat to pay attention to his cellphone vibrating. And he'd remained busy right up until a minute earlier. She must have assumed he'd just blown her off.

Bracing himself for her almost-certain rejection, he accessed his voicemail. She was going to tell him Curtis couldn't care for Draco any more. She wouldn't even bring up their potential date on Friday night.

"Hi, Rusty, this is Maya." Her tone, he noticed, was carefully neutral. "Curtis is doing fine. He's actually online right now looking up Belgian Malinois, if you can believe it. I guess that dog bite didn't put him off. In fact, he'd like to see Draco again whenever that works for you."

Amazement had him sinking back against his pillows.

"I just remembered that your guests came in this evening," she continued, "so you must be way too busy to pick up Curtis in the morning. If it's okay with you, I can bring him over in the afternoon when I get off work, and he could play with the dog for an hour or so—not to get paid; just to keep the bond going."

His heart started thumping with elation. Not only was she coming over tomorrow, but she hadn't cancelled their Friday date!

"If that's not okay, just let me know via text what your preference is. I know you're really busy. Okay, so, I guess I'll hear from you. Bye."

He texted back so fast that he had to type his reply three times to eliminate the typos.

Great idea. See you tomorrow afternoon.

Putting his phone back on the charger, he turned off the lights and yawned hugely into the darkness.

Draco's proximity filled him with a hankering to hold Maya close. The need to get to know her better had grown into a hungering in just a few days. If she bowed out of his life now, she would leave a void that might never be filled.

At zero three hundred hours, Rusty's phone vibrated with Maya's return text. Draco's snores drowned out the sound. Rusty read the message at zero five thirty in the morning the instant he woke up, and his smile was so wide it made his cheeks hurt.

We'll be by in the afternoon. See you around 4.

CHAPTER NINE

F ORGING RUSTY'S DRIVEWAY, Maya was struck by how lively the place looked compared to her previous visits. His property crawled with men. Some played Frisbee between the oak tree and the veranda while others peered under the hood of one of the many parked cars. Others stood on the dock out by the creek, holding fishing poles. At her approach, every man stopped what he was doing to assess whether she was friend or foe.

They were so fresh out of a war zone that their antennas were still set to high-alert. Ian had behaved the same way for the first week he was home, jumping at the least little sound. With half the men standing around bare-chested, she was glad she'd thought to change out of her work attire into shorts and a T-shirt. As she stepped out of her van, a dozen pairs of eyes skimmed over her slim, bare legs.

Through her affiliation with the Navy, she was used to being outnumbered by men, but these specimens weren't your average Joe—they were superhuman specimens of raw strength and intelligence. Just standing about in various postures of ease, they exuded physical readiness and supreme male confidence.

"Hello," she called to all within earshot, using just enough of her professional voice to send the message that she wasn't there to entertain them. She added a small general wave in no specific direction.

Undaunted, their stares conveyed enough appreciation of her femininity that her skin warmed and prickled. Some answered her greeting out loud. Others sent her come-hither smiles that reminded her they hadn't been around women in quite a long time.

But then Curtis pushed out of his side of the van, and taking stock of him, the SEALs came to conclusions about her availability and immediately looked away.

Just then Rusty strode around the corner and self-awareness swamped her again. With a look that expressed apology and a willingness to make amends, he closed the distance between them.

"Welcome back," he said, including Curtis in his greeting. "How's the ankle?"

"Better," Curtis answered, looking past him.

"Where's Draco?"

Rusty grimaced. "In his crate. He's a little freaked out right now with all the men around. When you take him out, please keep him on the lead, and don't give him too much slack."

Curtis nodded gravely. "Okay," he said, hurrying toward the far side of the house with just the slightest limp. He'd followed her orders to rest his ankle all morning while she was at work.

"Thank you for coming."

Rusty's words and warm look assured her their date that Friday was definitely on.

He tipped his auburn head. "Come on back," he invited, leading the way in the same direction that Curtis had taken.

At the rear of the house, still more men lobbed a volleyball back and forth over a tight, new net. One of them caught the ball so they could all turn and look at her.

Draco's excited barks shattered the quiet. Maya could see the dog was entirely fixated on Curtis, begging the boy to set him free. Her son crouched in front of the crate, telling the dog to hush with a soothing foreign word.

Rusty called out over the dog's noise. "Everyone, this is NCIS Special Investigator Maya Schultz and her son, Curtis."

As men called out greetings, Maya wondered

why Rusty had mentioned her title. Did he want the men to think their relationship was professional and not personal? Or did he want them keeping their distance because he meant to claim her for himself?

Seeing Curtis retrieve Draco's long lead, she watched with worry as he went to release the dog from his crate. Surely Draco wouldn't rush out and bite him again.

"You want to come in?" Rusty's invitation distracted her.

But she waited until Draco emerged with a lowered head and a wagging body before turning to follow.

"Place is a mess now that the men are here," he apologized, opening the door to the addition at the rear of the house.

Maya found herself in a huge farm-style kitchen with exposed crossbeams, a brick hearth, and lots of countertop space for prepping. To her, everything looked spic-and-span. The aroma of tomato soup and grilled cheese sandwiches still hung in the air. A member of the hired help Rusty had mentioned was putting clean dishes back into the tall oak cabinets.

"It's gorgeous," she exclaimed. Clearly the sponsors had believed in what he'd wanted to do and had helped him make it a wonderful reality.

"Let's go this way." He led her into the home's main structure to a seating area filled with leather couches, overstuffed chairs, and an enormous flat-screen TV.

"This is where we watch sports or movies," he confirmed. He waved her over to a door under the stairs. "Check out the waste bin you bought. Goes perfectly."

Peeking into the cream and beige bathroom, she had to admit that it did.

He took her past a glassed-in sunporch, a music area, an enormous formal dining room, and a library stuffed with books. "Is this your office?" she asked pointing out the desk with its neat piles of paper-work.

"Yeah, but I never get time to sit in there," he admitted. "Want to see the second floor?"

"Absolutely." What she'd seen so far epitomized good taste and functionality.

By the time they'd wandered through the second level and returned to the lower level via a steep staircase once used by servants, she had counted a total of eight bedrooms including Rusty's, each one of them attractive and inviting. A funny feeling had overcome her as she'd taken a mental snapshot of his queen-sized bed.

"Can I get you a drink?" Rusty asked as they reentered the kitchen. "Ginger ale, water?"

Between the heat outside and her tour of the house, she'd worked up a thirst. "Water would be great. Thanks."

As he filled a glass at the oversized refrigerator's dispenser, the question at the forefront of her mind formed on her lips.

"How on earth did you finance this place?"

He looked up at her in surprise.

She blushed at her own bluntness. "I'm sorry. It's none of my business. You've done a great job here, and the entire thing looks top quality. It had to have cost a bundle."

"No, it's fine," he assured her. He gestured to the long plank table. "Want to sit?"

They sat catty-corner from each other with Rusty at the end. "My father passed away last year," he began.

She searched his fascinating face with its subtle lines of suffering and too much sun. "I'm so sorry. He couldn't have been very old," she guessed.

"Sixty-six," he confirmed. "He'd delivered produce all his life, since boyhood. His father, my grandfather, fled Poland during World War II. *Dziadek* started the family business, and my father took it over. I still have the van he used to drive."

She nodded, remembering how he'd loaned it to Bronco the previous fall.

"They would pick up the fruits and vegetables from farms all over New Jersey and bring them to grocers in Orange. Dad did that for fifty years. All his life, he talked about where he would live when he retired—out in the country somewhere. He saved every penny he could. When my mother was killed in a train wreck, he was compensated by Amtrak, and he invested that money, intending to buy a farmhouse and renovate it. But he never got the chance. All the pollution blowing in from Newark had given him lung cancer. He died only six months after he was diagnosed."

His gruff tone inspired her sympathy, bringing tears to her eyes. "I'm so sorry," she murmured. She looked around. "And now you've made his dream come true."

He acknowledged her statement with a bitter-sweet smile. "With a little twist of my own."

The urge to lean across the table and kiss him got the better of her. She'd been wanting to know what it would feel like, so why not just do it?

As she inclined her face toward his, Curtis burst into the house through the mudroom with the dog in tow.

"Hey, I have an idea," he said excitedly.

Rusty cast him a tolerant look. "What's that?"

"Draco thinks, with all the guys here, that we're going on a mission. That's why he's so pumped up. These dogs are made to work. So let's give him a job and plant some explosives in the woods. I'll bet you he can find them!"

Explosives? Maya started to protest the idea, but Rusty cut her off.

"That's actually a really good idea."

"It is?" she asked.

He shot out of his chair. "I know some guys who'd love to help. Come on, let's go ask them."

Feeling forgotten, Maya just sat in her chair.

Rusty disappeared into the mudroom, then doubled back. "You coming?" he asked.

"Sure." She chugged a few sips of her water and got up to follow.

"ALL RIGHT, MEN, listen up."

The command in Rusty's voice inspired Maya's immediate respect. His tone beckoned rather than bullied. The man about to serve the volleyball tucked it under his arm as all eyes swung toward Rusty, and all mouths snapped shut. He had their undivided attention.

"We're going to put the dog through a training exercise—bury weapons in the woods and see if he can find them." Crossing to a wooden storage bench, he withdrew a container full of tennis balls. Pulling the lid off, he upended the balls into the bench, emptying the bucket.

"Anyone willing to surrender a weapon, just drop it in here. If the dog finds the cache within half an hour, we'll tap a keg of beer tonight. If not, you'll wait until the weekend."

He carried the bucket to the middle of the yard and, holding onto the lid, backed away from it. "Your call, of course."

Maya watched as the men looked at each other, waiting for someone to make the first move. Where were these weapons supposed to come from?

Turning his back on the bucket, Rusty walked in her direction while sending her a wink. "Be right back," he said, continuing toward the oversized shed beyond the parked cars.

Savoring the wink, which conveyed a deeper intimacy between them than what they'd shared up until now, she watched him walk away. From his broad shoulders to his tight butt encased in denim shorts to the well-formed calf muscles that bunched and released, his physical aspect filled her with desire.

From the corner of her eye, she noted several men approaching the bucket with pistols in their hands. Her eyes widened at the realization that they'd been carrying those firearms under their clothing. With rising astonishment, she watched several more weapons come into view. Nearly every man in sight was packing heat—what the hell? And she was letting her son frolic in this environment? Was she crazy?

Watching the SEALs take turns laying their arms

every-so-gently into the bucket, however, she reminded herself that these men were professionals. They ate, slept, and trained with their weapons day after day without hurting anyone but the enemy. She had to trust that they'd take extra precautions with a civilian in the area, a teenager at that.

By the time Rusty reappeared, carrying a shovel in one hand, the bucket was so full, he struggled to get the lid back on.

He straightened to assess his audience—their game of volleyball forgotten. All eyes were glued to Draco, who stood on the other end of the leash Curtis was holding, his eyes bright with excitement and his tail whipping happily back and forth.

"Now, who wants to bury the bucket in the woods?" Rusty asked. When every man present raised a hand, Curtis laughed. Maya took note of his anticipation. These motivated men were good role models for her son. So what if they were armed and dangerous? They were no threat to Curtis—only to terrorists and extremists.

"Yogi and Weinstein."

Receiving cheers from their comrades, two men separated from the group. One snatched up the bucket and the other took the shovel. Grinning ear to ear, they headed for the woods at a run with encouragement from those left behind. The faster the weapons were buried, the sooner the dog could find the cache, the more chance they'd all be drinking beer that night.

"You okay?"

Rusty's question wrested her attention to his searching gaze.

"Yeah." She sent him a reassuring smile.

"Disturbed to see so much firepower in my backyard?"

"I was taken aback," she admitted, glancing at Curtis to convey her reasons.

"You don't have to worry," he assured her.

"I'm not worried."

"Good." He gestured to her son. "Let me work with Curtis on the search procedure."

"By all means."

For the next ten minutes, she watched her son learn to guide Draco through the search. He would give the command "*reveire*," while keeping Draco on the lead but with as much slack as possible. When the dog located the bucket by the scent of gunpowder, he would sit and stare at the site.

"He won't try to dig it up?" Curtis asked.

"No, no. You wouldn't want the dog digging up something that might explode, would you?"

Horror registered on Curtis's face. "Oh, no," he said.

"Our explosives guy will dig up the bucket. There's a chance this boy may not even find it. His nose isn't what it used to be. If that happens, we'll have to plant something back here at the house or he'll lose motivation."

"Right." Caught up in the moment, Curtis stroked Draco's head enthusiastically.

A shout went up across the field signaling the return of the two SEALs. They waved the shovel in the air to show that the bucket was buried.

"Let's do this." Rusty swung back toward Maya. "Want to join us?"

"Of course."

His gaze dubiously slid to her slip-on sandals.

"I'll be fine," she assured him.

He turned back to Curtis. "You take point, son. That means you're first. Our safety now rests in the hands of you and your MWD."

Curtis smiled uncertainly. "Draco," he called, dropping all but the end of the long lead, "reviere!"

The dog leapt into action. He started forward in a zigzag pattern, unraveling his lead as he alternately lifted his head to scent the air then lowered it to sniff the ground.

Conditioned by their training and experience, the men fell in automatically after him, one of them snatching the shovel out of Weinstein's hand. Maya joined them, hurrying to keep up as they tramped across the field and into the tree line. Rusty slowed his step to walk beside her, a suggestion of a smile on his rugged face.

As they stepped into the forest, he put a hand on her elbow. "Watch your step."

His light but reassuring grip sent an electric charge crackling up her arm.

Pine needles crunched beneath her sandals, but she could barely hear Rusty's footfalls as he drifted almost silently alongside her.

"Is this land yours, too?" she asked, taking in the freshly made path. Peering past the few SEALs ahead of them, she kept on eye on Curtis's sun-dappled shoulders as he trotted in the dog's wake, trying to prevent the lead from tangling in the undergrowth.

"Thirty-three acres," Rusty affirmed.

"It's so peaceful," she stated.

Just then, a couple of birds startled out of the trees up ahead, and the SEALs around them snapped into defensive postures before recovering with sheepish expressions.

Rusty slanted her a look. "Forty-eight hours ago, they were being mortared," he quietly explained.

At his words, she regarded the warriors with fresh eyes. This sort of exercise wasn't just a game to them; it was a way of life. Their stealth and height-ened awareness inspired her respect. One man held a branch for her so it wouldn't catch her in the face.

She smiled and thanked him.

"Watch your step on these roots," Rusty warned as they came to a spot where water had eroded the soil.

They arrived at a ravine. The dog had already forded it, disappearing over the opposite rise with Curtis scrambling to keep up. The SEALs behind him leapt over the stream and surged up the hill like it wasn't there. To Maya's astonishment, Rusty swept her off her feet before she had a chance to get her sandals wet.

Held aloft, against the breadth of his chest, she suffered no concern that he would drop her as he waded through the ravine, soaking his sneakers without so much as a grimace. Then he put her down, grabbed her hand and pulled her up the rise with ease.

Flustered by the brief, close contact, her heart continued to beat erratically. Their gazes met then skittered away, leaving her breathless.

It's just a matter of time until I sleep with him, she realized.

Caught up in thoughts of their inevitable intimacy, Maya lost track of both time and distance. This wasn't going to become some lighthearted romance that she would enjoy for a time and leave behind. This was something real, something permanent. Her heart thrummed like an engine with a fresh set of spark plugs. *Am I ready for this?*

Draco's sudden bark pulled her out of her intro-spection.

"He found it," exclaimed the SEAL holding the shovel.

Searching for Curtis, Maya found him standing over Draco, who sat staring fixedly at a pile of sticks and leaves several feet from the path. The area looked completely natural and undisturbed. How could the bucket be hidden there?

"Everybody stand back," Rusty ordered, speaking quite obviously to Curtis, who hovered over the pile. "If there were explosives buried here, you and Draco would want to be fifty feet away right now. Since we're dealing with a stash of weapons, fifteen feet is good enough."

Curtis backed up and joined the ring of men en-circling the area.

"It's your baby, Higgins," Rusty said, and the man with the shovel approached the pile of debris.

"Higgins is a demolition expert," Rusty added in Maya's ear. "It's his job to identify and neutralize IEDs."

Watching Higgins scrape the leaves and sticks off to one side using the end of the shovel, Maya pictured him scraping through rock and sand, putting his life on the line in search of wires or pressure plates.

God bless you, she thought, as he sank his shovel

into the soft dirt and tossed it gingerly to one side.

As Higgins dug deeper with nothing to show for it, several onlookers started to comment that the dog must have screwed up. No way was the bucket buried more than a foot in the ground. Higgins had already dug that deep.

"Soil's soft," Higgins assured them. "This is the place."

"Draco's done this too many times to be wrong," Curtis stated, putting his faith in the dog.

One look at Draco's bright eyes and quivering snout, and Maya had to agree with her son.

The sound of the shovel striking plastic brought an exclamation of triumph from the onlookers. Higgins reached down, grabbed the buried object, and pulled out the bucket.

Curtis dropped to his knees and threw his arms around Draco's neck. "*Braaf,* Draco!" He scrubbed the dog's head as he praised him. "*Braaf!*"

With the dog's teeth so close to Curtis's face, Maya tensed with sudden concern, but then Draco turned his head and licked Curtis's face. The dog appeared to be smiling. Suddenly she knew Curtis was right—he and the dog had bonded. There'd be no more bites to worry about from here on.

Higgins had pried the lid off the bucket and was doling out the various wicked-looking handguns. Their owners were quick to reclaim their firearms, making Maya guess the SEALs had probably felt hugely vulnerable without them, even for that short period of time.

"What do you think?"

Turning her head, she caught Rusty regarding her profile intently.

"I'm impressed," she admitted. "And not only with the dog." She held his gaze, letting her admiration for him show.

His coppery eyebrows shot up. "Me?" he asked. "I get brownie points?"

"You do."

"For what?" he asked.

"For everything." She kept her reasons to herself—no need to give the man a big head. But she'd seen firsthand why his men revered him. He looked out for others—not just for their physical welfare but for their mental and emotional health.

He'd looked out for Curtis and he was looking out for her, too. Everything about Rusty was too good to be true. Or were her feelings for him blinding her to some fault she couldn't see?

Shaking off her doubts, she focused on their upcoming date. Time would tell.

CHAPTER TEN

PULLING INTO A parking space in front of Maya's condo, Rusty wondered if he shouldn't have bought himself a new car instead of pouring all his money into Never Forget Retreat. Luckily, Maya wasn't the type to kick him to the curb just because he drove a beater.

Two days had passed since Draco showed off his ferreting capabilities. His guests at the retreat had settled into their various therapeutic activities, while Curtis kept Draco entertained and out of their way. Morning and afternoon, Rusty had enjoyed brief conversations with Maya as she dropped off or picked up her son. At long last it was Friday, and here he was, collecting her for their long-awaited date on the beach.

Having arrived typically early, he spared a thought for his appearance, wondering if his cargo shorts and yellow-collared polo weren't too dressy.

Blowing out a calming breath, he eyed the hazy sky and prayed that the clouds edging the horizon would keep away so they could enjoy their bonfire.

As he headed for Maya's front door, it sprang open and out stepped Curtis looking slightly sunburned from having taken Draco down the creek in a dinghy that day.

Their gazes met, and Curtis's face reflected puzzlement and then surprise.

"Oh." He looked at Rusty as if seeing him for the first time. "Mom's going out with *you*?" he asked.

Rusty blinked at the odd question. "She didn't tell you?"

"No." And given the look on Curtis's face, the thought of the two adults hooking up had never occurred to him.

Annoyance flashed through Rusty, followed by concern. Why wouldn't Maya have told her son she planned to date Rusty—unless she didn't think their date would lead to anything permanent? Uncertainty ambushed him.

"Well, I hope it's okay with you," he said, desirous of the boy's blessing. Crap, if Curtis said no, he'd have to get in his car and drive away. His heart thudded as he awaited judgment.

Curtis shrugged. He scratched his ear. "Sure, I guess. Who's watching Draco?"

The boy's concern for the dog warmed Rusty.

"Couple of the guys volunteered to keep him close tonight. One of them knew Nichols, Draco's former handler."

"Oh, cool." Mentioning Nichols made Curtis reflect a moment. "As long as he's not stuck in his crate all evening," he added.

"Nope. They're going to keep him on his lead. What about you? Where're you going?" It occurred to Rusty that Curtis would be on his own while they were at the beach.

"A friend's house. Mom says I can buy one new video game with some of the money you gave me, but I'm going to save the rest," he promised.

"Good man. And I didn't give you any money; you earned it." Clapping a hand on Curtis's shoulder, he noted the density of the boy's growing bones. "Remember you've got a good head on your shoulders. Make sure you use it tonight."

"Yes, sir."

Rusty let his hand fall. "I've never been a sir," he reminded Curtis. "Your father was the officer. I'm just a retired, enlisted man."

Curtis regarded him thoughtfully. Rusty could practically see him contrasting what he knew of his father to what he saw in Rusty. "Right, sorry," he apologized.

"No problem. You have a good night."

"Thanks." Leaning back inside the door, Curtis

bellowed, "I'm leaving, Mom!"

"Be home by ten." Maya's return shout came from the back room.

The boy edged past him. "See you later, Rusty."

At last, the kid had called him by name. Rusty hid a smile. "See you."

Curtis bounded off the stoop and hurried up the sidewalk. Stepping through the door the boy had left open, Rusty shut it quietly behind him and made his way to the kitchen. Likely Maya didn't even know he was here. Glancing toward her bedroom door, which stood slightly ajar, he glimpsed her bare back and bra strap as she threaded her arms through the sleeves of a T-shirt.

The thrill that chased through him made him wonder if he'd get to pull that T-shirt off her later.

Easy, he cautioned himself. Maya wasn't the type of woman to fall into bed on a first date. From what he could glean of the past ten years, she hadn't even dated at all after being widowed. Hell, he'd be lucky if she even let him kiss her.

She turned, suddenly, still tugging her T-shirt into place and started visibly at the sight of him standing outside her door.

"How long have you been here?" she demanded, reaching out to pull it all the way open.

He sent her a sheepish grin. "Sorry. Didn't mean to startle you. I came in when Curtis left."

"Oh." Her hands stilled over her abdomen. "Then he saw you," she realized.

His smile faded. "Yes." He let the implications settle before adding, "I asked him if I could take you out tonight. He said it was okay."

The tight skin on her face relaxed. "He did?"

"How come you didn't tell him we were going out?" If she wasn't serious about the two of them, then he wouldn't waste her time.

Her gaze jumped away. "I meant to." She looked around at the floor behind her, possibly looking for her shoes. Disappearing briefly, she came out in a denim skirt, pale green T-shirt, and sandals.

"You look about twenty years old," he inserted, unable to stop smiling.

She looked away with a self-conscious blush. "I meant to tell Curtis," she repeated. "It's just . . . I didn't get the chance." Silver bracelets jangled on her wrist as she lifted a hand to adjust her hair. But she couldn't look him in the eye.

"You ready?" he asked, unwilling to probe her feelings if she wasn't ready to admit to them.

"Almost." She brushed past him to get to the refrigerator and a tantalizing fragrance floated into his nostrils, rekindling his ardor. "I've got something to contribute." Pulling a bottle of wine from the refrigerator, she showed it to him. "My favorite *pinot grigio*. Do you mind if we bring it?"

"Of course not." He'd tucked a bottle of zinfandel into the cooler, but the zin could keep.

"Plus a snack," she added, producing a baggie filled with freshly cut vegetables.

"Great." It would go with the cheese and crackers he'd packed.

"Do I need to bring anything—a towel, beach chairs?" She shut the refrigerator.

"I've got everything we need," he said.

"Of course you do." She cast him a teasing smile. "I forgot whom I was talking to."

"It's going to be okay, Maya," he heard himself assure her. "We're going to have fun."

To his astonished dismay, her eyes grew suddenly bright and her nose turned pink. She stood still a second, clearly fighting to retain her composure.

"I'm sorry. I'm really out of practice," she said in a strained voice.

"Please don't apologize." A vision of her dead husband, guts strewn across the rocks he lay atop, flashed across the backs of his eyes. "We can talk about Ian tonight," he suggested, "if you want to."

It was the dead last thing *he* wanted to do, but if they were going to put the past behind them, then they needed to remember the dead man and ask for his blessing.

She visibly brightened. "Okay," she agreed.

CURTIS TURNED A puzzled gaze toward the parking lot, wondering where his friend Matt might be. They were supposed to hang out, maybe even walk all the way to the shopping center to buy a copy of a new PS4 game. But not only was Matt not home, his family car was missing.

Curtis teased his mom's old cellphone out of his pocket. The stupid thing didn't even get data. *Where are you?* he texted Matt.

Late afternoon sun beat down on him. He batted away a pesky fly as he waited. Finally, Matt texted him back.

Sorry. Forgot about my soccer game. Won't be home till eight.

Curtis's shoulders slumped. His mom would kill him if he walked to the store alone. She'd been especially protective lately, telling him to keep the door locked and not to answer to any strangers.

He thought about his other friends. Jason was on vacation, which only left Santana, whom his mom didn't like. But Mom wasn't around that evening, so why not hang out with him? She would never know the difference.

He thought about Lucifer, Santana's uncle's dog. The big Doberman didn't scare him anymore—not after Draco. Rusty had taught Curtis to project his inner alpha. If he did that, the dog wouldn't try to intimidate him.

Making up his mind, he trotted toward Santana's front door and knocked, a little disappointed when no dog barked and Santana's mother, who looked exhausted with her lank, blond hair escaping its bun, opened the door.

"Oh, hey," she said. She held the door open wider. "Santana's in his room. You can go on up."

Curtis caught Santana stuffing a magazine under his bed. He didn't ask what kind it was.

"Hey, I made some money with my job," he announced. "You want to come with me to Game Stop and buy the *Carmageddon* game?"

Santana leapt off his bed. "How much you got?"

Curtis was glad he'd left most of his money at home. "Forty bucks. I think it only costs thirty-five."

"Cool. Let's go." Crossing to his dresser, Santana slid what looked like a penlight and a screwdriver into the rear pocket of his sagging jeans.

Curtis racked his brains but couldn't think why Santana would need either item. Not wanting to appear stupid, he didn't ask.

They thundered down the stairs together. Without a word to his mother, Santana led him straight out of the house and into the muggy evening air. They turned in the direction of the shopping area situated a mile and a half from the condominium complex. Curtis glanced at the sky, now edged by a wall of dark storm clouds. If they hurried, they could get to the store and back before it started raining. The hum of traffic on the main road beckoned them.

Santana suddenly stopped walking. "Hey, you want to see something cool?" he asked Curtis.

"Like what?"

"You'll see." Santana's light-hued eyes gleamed with mystery. "Come on," he urged. Stepping off the sidewalk, he headed toward the trees that backed the condominium complex.

Glancing at his friend's rear pocket, Curtis followed with some reluctance. Santana wouldn't skewer him for forty dollars, would he?

"Where are we going?"

He'd been in these woods several times over the years. There was nothing back there but a utility road and a creek that filled with water whenever it rained.

Santana didn't answer him. His gaze darted left and right as if he were worried about being seen.

Another thought occurred to Curtis. "You're not going to smoke pot back here or something, are you?" Maybe his mother's assessment of Santana hadn't been all that far off.

His friend cast a frown of annoyance in his direction. "No, man. I don't smoke pot." He leaped over a log, and Curtis was forced to follow.

"So what are we doing then?" he persisted.

"Shhh." Santana hushed him. "Keep quiet. Let me know if you hear anything."

All Curtis heard was the twitter of song birds and a pair of squirrels scampering up the trunk of a tree. The soft ground began to slope downward as they neared the area where run-off from the streets poured into a stream. When they came upon the little tributary, Curtis spotted the mouth of a large storm drain, big enough to walk into if you hunched over. Santana was heading straight toward it.

"We're not going in there, are we?" Curtis asked.

His friend grinned at him then ducked his head and walked into the opening.

Curtis drew up short, eying the dark maw with mistrust.

Santana came back to the opening. "Trust me. You're gonna want to see this."

"See what?"

Scanning the forest with his light eyes, Santana leaned out of the storm drain and murmured, "Guns. Rifles. Lots of 'em."

"Seriously?" Curtis didn't believe him.

"Come on. I'll show you."

Sparing a thought for his cellphone and whether he ought to send his mom a text first, Curtis decided he had better not.

Cool, moist air blew into his face as he joined

Santana in the cement cylinder. The tunnel smelled of stale water and car oil. Luckily, it hadn't rained lately, and water trickled in a narrow stream between his feet. He could straddle the trickle and avoid getting his sneakers wet.

When the tunnel grew too dark, Santana paused and snapped on his penlight. So that was why he'd brought it along. Unable to see past his taller friend's shoulders, Curtis fixed his gaze on the debris littering the bottom of the tunnel—cans and bottles and plastic bags.

They had walked about fifty feet when the tunnel crossed another one just like it, offering them three ways to go. Santa turned to the right. "Almost there," he said.

Curtis couldn't ignore the rising certainty that they were asking for trouble. "We ought to go back," he insisted, slowing his step.

Santana glanced over his shoulder at him. "You gonna be a pussy when we've come this far?"

"Shut up," Curtis ordered, giving him a shove.

"It's right up here, anyway." Santana's voice echoed in the chamber. "Look." He shone his light along the wall, and Curtis caught sight of a grill at knee level blocking the entrance to a smaller tunnel. A lock, shiny and new, kept the grill shut. As Santana approached it pulling out his screwdriver, Curtis wondered if he wasn't telling the truth, after all.

Ignoring the lock, Santana popped the penlight between his teeth and applied his screwdriver to the hinges on the other side. When the screws lifted right out, Curtis realized Santana had done this before. He dropped the screws into his pocket, gave the grill a yank, and pulled it off its hinges. Leaving it dangling by the lock, he reached into the eighteen-inch opening, grabbed hold of something that sounded heavy as Santana dragged it closer. Then he swung the object into the bigger tunnel and shone his penlight down so Curtis could see.

What he saw was a big plastic container like the kind sold in Walmart for storing wrapping paper.

"Go ahead," Santana invited, on a told-you-so note. "Open it."

"Is it full of snakes or something?"

"I told you. Guns."

"No way."

"Yep. And there's another one just like it." He nodded at the opening. "Lift the lid."

His friend's confidence had Curtis tugging off the snug-fitting lid. Santana angled his light under the covering so he could see.

Curtis's eyes widened. He'd seen something similar just the other day—a bucket filled with all kinds of handguns. This was exactly the same, only the container was longer, the guns were bigger, and there were a lot more of them.

"These are all AR-15s," Santana said, picking up one of them and hefting it in the crook of his arm. "The other box is full of M-4s. I looked them up. You know how much one of these babies goes for? They're two grand apiece, man. We must be lookin' at fifty thousand dollars sittin' right here!"

A shiver traced Curtis's spine. "Don't point that at me. How'd they get here?" he wanted to know.

"I don't know," Santana answered a tad too quickly.

"How'd you find them?" Curtis pressed.

Santana pretended to aim the rifle at him. "Don't worry about it. Promise me you won't tell nobody."

"I promise," he said, quickly.

Satisfied, Santana swung the rifle over his shoulder and pressed the lid tightly onto the plastic tub.

"You're going to take that?" Curtis's question came out in an embarrassing falsetto.

"Big deal. It's just one. They got like thirty here."

"You need to put it back," Curtis insisted.

"Don't tell me what to do. You just jealous 'cause you don't have one. Here, hold this," he added, thrusting the rifle at Curtis while he heaved the big box back into the smaller tunnel.

Recoiling from the gun he was holding, Curtis wondered if he could go to jail for this. These guns had to be stolen and now his fingerprints were on this one.

Santana jammed the grate back onto its hinges and threaded the screws back in their holes with nimble fingers. He tightened down the screws with his screwdriver.

"We gonna wait 'til it's dark," he said, putting it away and grabbing the rifle out of Curtis's slack grip. "Then I'll walk home and hide it in my room."

"What are you going to do with it?"

"Sell it. Watchu think?"

"How?" Curtis asked.

"On the internet, dumbass. Come on, let's get out of here."

All too eager to exit the dank enclosure, Curtis turned and started blindly forward. His toe struck a can which ricocheted loudly off the cement wall before splashing into water. They arrived at the place where the pipes intersected, and he turned left, relieved to see a glimmer of daylight up ahead.

Perhaps he should tell his mom about Santana's discovery. He didn't want his friend getting into trouble, but these weapons were proof of a crime, and even though his mom didn't work civilian cases, he'd been taught the value of evidence when it came to convicting bad guys.

Yep, as soon as he was alone again, he would text her. Rusty would bring her home right away—Curtis knew him well enough to know that. What he'd seen tonight was freaking him out.

CHAPTER ELEVEN

STARING INTO THE leaping flames of their bonfire, Maya listened to Rusty's rendition of the horrific battle that had claimed Ian's life. With the wine they'd shared loosening his tongue, he divulged more than he otherwise might have, she was sure, explaining why the Marines had been sent up Gilman Ridge in the first place—to rescue an Army Corporal who had wandered away from his battalion and been grabbed by the Taliban.

It was supposed to have been a quick and easy rescue, but Intelligence had failed the Marines, causing her husband's platoon to stumble into an enemy force ten times the size of their own. The only support close enough to help in a timely fashion had been Rusty's squad consisting of four SEALs who'd just completed their own mission.

"And so we created a diversion, hoping to draw attention away from the Marines and onto us,"

Rusty added. "What happened, instead, was that another wave of Taliban came running out of some caves to the east, and we were caught squarely in the middle, with no way out. The Marines took a heavy toll, and one of my guys sustained a chest wound. The Taliban pounded us with rocket launchers, grenades, gunfire, everything they had. They mortared the hell out of us, until we all ended up in the same place, behind an outcrop of boulders."

Picturing it in her mind's eye, a lump grew in Maya's throat. The breeze blowing in off the ocean dried her tears before they could fall.

"Would you like me to stop?" he asked, his voice gravely with emotion.

It couldn't be any easier for him to relive the event than it was for her to hear about it, but she shook her head all the same. "If you can talk about it, then I want to know." She wasn't sure it was for the best for Rusty to dwell on the horrors he'd lived through, but she felt she owed it to Ian to know what he'd gone through.

Rusty pressed on. "When our gunner was hit in the head, I figured we'd be overrun within minutes." His gruff voice seemed to blend with the roar of the waves crashing and retreating only yards away. "But then Ian took over the M240 machine gun, and I'd never seen anyone fire that weapon with such precision. Our rounds were running out. Every bullet had to count. He must have cut the enemy in half. Suddenly, we actually had a chance of holding out until the air support could reach us.

"By then there were just seven of us left with the others dead or bleeding out all around us. The extraction helicopter was within sight when a grenade came bouncing down the hill. And damn if it didn't roll right into the space where the seven of us were holed up. It landed closest to Ian. I expected him to snatch it up and toss it over the boulders, but he knew how long it had been rolling. He knew there wasn't time. He looked right at me with this resolve that I'll never forget. And then he threw himself face down on top of it."

The picture in her mind was so vivid, Maya clapped her hands over her eyes. The pain that had lessened over the years returned with the same devastating force that had leveled her when she'd been informed of her husband's death. If not for Curtis, who'd been four at the time, she might have sunk irreparably into depression. Instead, she'd kept busy, and day by day, year by year, her loss got easier.

Rusty's shoulder brushed hers, letting her know that he'd shifted closer. His powerful arm encircled her, drawing her gently to him. Her shoulder fit neatly under his arm. With Ian's countenance still fresh in her mind's eye, she turned toward Rusty's offer of consolation and pressed her face against his neck, breathing his fresh sage scent. Laying her hand against his chest, she registered the steady thump of his heart, taking comfort from it.

"I'm sorry," he said into her ear.

It was oddly comforting to know that Rusty had been there in Ian's last moments. She'd known about Ian sacrificing himself to save the others. But she'd never thought to consider that if the grenade had rolled next to Rusty, he'd have done the exact same thing. She now knew he would have. And knowing that made it impossible to resent him for surviving. Ian had wanted the other men to make it out.

She lifted her head abruptly. "Wait, what happened to the others?"

Rusty's gaze swung toward the horizon, already swallowed up in darkness. His thumb stroked her upper arm absently as his thoughts traveled to another place and time. "Two caught bullets right after Ian died. The others were hit by shrapnel when a mortar blew up behind us on our way to the helo. I got them all onto the Blackhawk, but they didn't survive the blast."

She envisioned the risks he'd taken to try and save the last four. What an awful burden to have been the lone survivor.

Realizing that their mouths were only inches

apart, Maya succumbed to the urge to comfort him. She leaned closer, closed her eyes, and touched her mouth to his.

His lips molded warmly to hers. Heat and desire flooded her instantly as their mouths slowly fused. His tongue stroked between her parted lips, and she lost herself to the wave of desire that crashed over her, pulling her into an undertow so fierce that she forgot to breathe.

She'd spent a decade in a sexual drought, lonely and—yes—resentful that death had taken her husband and life partner from her. Suddenly, her heart and body were being quenched at the same time, making the drought seem worthwhile in the face of such a sweet reawakening.

"WHAT'VE WE GOT here?"

The unexpected question startled Curtis into backing up. He collided with Santana, who held the AR-15 across his chest as he followed on Curtis's heels.

Three dark figures detached themselves from the tunnel wall, blocking the light of the exit. In the next instant a flashlight flared to life, pinning him and Santana in its blinding beam.

Curtis raised an arm to shield his eyes, and the pale face of a stranger, followed by two more men, one harder to see than the other, swam out of the darkness.

"Santana!" the darkest figure exclaimed. "What the hell you doin' here?"

Curtis recognized the pitch and dialect of Santana's uncle. A modicum of relief slowed his pounding heart.

"He's helping himself to our stash, is what he's doing," the first man accused in an angry voice. Shoving Curtis out of his way, he snatched the AR-15 out of Santana's grasp. Then he grabbed Santana by the scruff. "You know this kid?" he asked, turning to Will.

Santana's uncle heaved a sigh. "He's my nephew. He must have followed us the other day."

"You followed us?" the man demanded, giving Santana a shake.

"Yeah," Santana admitted, his voice suddenly tremulous.

The man's eyes glittered in the dark as he assessed the situation. Curtis made out a thin scar at the corner of his mouth.

"Grab the other kid, Will," he ordered. The scar made it look like he was leering. "They've seen our stash. We can't let them leave."

His ruthless words penetrated Curtis's consciousness slowly. By the time Uncle Will siezed his arm, it was too late to bolt past the two men blocking his way and run for it. What had Scarface meant by *can't let them leave?*

"Come on, Tom. They ain't gonna tell no one," Uncle Will protested.

"Shut up, you idiot. You just told them my name. You think with the investigation going on we can afford to let them go? You *are* a stupid mother fucker."

Uncle Will seemed to expand in size, shrinking the narrow space. "Don't you talk that way to me. I'm the one who came up with a place to hide our shit. If we did things your way, we'd be sittin' in jail right now."

"Yeah, great hiding place," the third man scoffed. Spanning the tunnel with his arms, he blocked the only escape route. "It's so good that a couple of kids managed to find it."

"Listen," Will insisted. "Santana is family. Let him go, and I promise you, he'll keep his mouth shut." His tone implied that he'd personally see to that. "But the other kid just happens to be the son of the investigator working for NCIS."

Startled to hear his mother mentioned, Curtis met Uncle Will's dark, glittering gaze.

"No shit!" Scar-faced Tom turned his flashlight onto Curtis, who flinched from the glare. "He's that Schultz bitch's son?"

The lanky third man let his arms drop slowly.

Curtis sucked in a sharp breath. What did that guy just call his mom?

"I told you she lived just up the road from me," Uncle Will said.

"Well, shit," Tom breathed. "Ain't that something?"

The sour taste of dread filled Curtis's mouth as he realized the untenable situation he was in. His mother had to be investigating these men. That made him a very serious liability. Even if they moved their stash of weapons somewhere else, Curtis had heard enough to testify against them. The only way to avoid answering for their crimes was to make sure Curtis never told anyone—which meant they were going to *kill* him.

He fought the sudden, overwhelming need to urinate.

"So what do we do?" The third man asked, his tone conveying a clear reluctance to do anything drastic.

"We shoot him and leave him here," Tom proposed.

"Please," Curtis whispered, about to embarrass himself.

"He won't tell anyone," Santana insisted.

Tom ignored them both. "We shoot him dead," he continued. "It's the only way to guarantee his silence."

"Now look," Uncle Will's tone became serious. "It's one thing to smuggle guns. It's a whole 'nother thing to kill somebody. I don't want no part of this."

"Me neither," piped up the third man.

Curtis held his breath while praying for deliverance.

"Then what do you suggest?" Tom mocked. "We've made it this far. NCIS has nothing on us. We're practically in the clear. We let them out of here, this one'll go running to his mother. Even if we move our stash, his testimony alone would sink us."

A thoughtful silence filled the chamber. Curtis overheard a distant rumble of thunder.

"So we lock this one in."

Will's suggestion turned Curtis's blood to icewater. He glanced at Santana, who fixed his wide eyes on Curtis and said nothing. "I promise, I won't tell anyone," he swore, wishing his voice hadn't cracked.

"Shut up," Tom bit out. "Lock him up where?"

"Where we hid the boxes," Will continued. "We gotta move them now anyway."

"What if he crawls up the tunnel and gets out?"

"Number one, he won't fit. Number two, that line leads to one place and there ain't no way out of it. I saw to that. He'll be trapped in there. Ain't no one going to hear him yellin' for help, neither. In a few days, he'll die on his own."

Curtis's legs threatened to give out. They wouldn't really leave him locked behind the grate, would they? He suddenly remembered his cellphone and hope bolstered his quaking knees. He just had to hide it before they realized what he had.

"Where can we put the stash?" asked the third man.

"I'll put the tubs in the crawlspace at my sister's until we find something better," Will offered.

"No, I'll take them," Tom decided. "That way your nephew won't be helping himself." He sent Santana a hard glare. "You'd better not say a word, kid, or I'll kill you myself," he threatened.

Caught in the cone of the flashlight's yellow glow, Santana's eyes resembled underwater pools. He shook his head, unable to speak.

"He won't talk," Uncle Will said with absolute conviction.

"All right then." Tom wrestled Santana in the opposite direction. "Time to put this rifle back with the others," he said.

Uncle Will swung Curtis around, propelling him on weak legs to follow.

As they moved deeper into the sewers, Curtis slipped his fingers into his pocket and pulled out his cheap flip phone, hastily shoving it under the waistband of his pants and into his underwear. For the first time ever, he was glad his mom still bought him uncool tighty-whities.

These men were going to lock him into a narrow, concrete pipe thinking they would leave him there to die. Hah. He'd call 9-1-1 as soon as they left, and he'd be free by nightfall.

I'm going to be okay, he assured himself.

CHAPTER TWELVE

SUMMONING HIS SELF-RESTRAINT, Rusty pressed Maya gently back upon the towel he'd spread across the sand. She lay back, her skin luminescent in the fire's glow, her eyes wide with wonder. The dark sky overhead gave a rumble that reflected the desire fulminating in Rusty's bloodstream. Bracing his weight on one elbow, he lay next to her in lieu of stretching his body over hers. A gentleman never took advantage on the first date.

Her kisses would suffice.

As he'd imagined from the moment he'd met her, her lips were heaven to kiss. She tasted of the mellow wine they'd imbibed, and she responded with a willingness that humbled him, taking off her glasses and setting them in the sand.

Mesmerized by the pale depths of her green eyes, he gave a groan of hunger as he fastened his mouth to hers. With his free hand, he stroked, the indentation of her narrow waist and the sweet flare of her hips, stopping short of palming the swells of her breasts or, better yet, sliding his fingers up under her skirt toward the heated juncture of her thighs.

And before he took this any further, he owed it to her to be completely honest, confessing something that might send her running in the opposite direction.

Ending the kiss with reluctance, he drew a deep breath to diminish his lust. He cleared his throat. "I need to tell you something.

She blinked up at him, and the film of desire lifted from her eyes.

Did he really have to do this? The last thing he wished to do right then was scare her off. He queried his conscience one last time. Yes, he did. She deserved to know what she was getting into.

"I've seen a lot of men die, Maya. Whether it's the death of an enemy or a colleague, it makes no difference. They're all human beings."

She nodded slowly, searching his face as if it were a mysterious map.

He pressed on. "When you're with people you care about in the moment that they cross over, it's like . . . you're in a holy place. That's the only way I know to describe it. It's holy the way church is, only it's scary as hell."

Her gaze took on an anxious quality, but she

kept quiet, clearly sensing he had more to say.

"Sometimes, the men I've been with at death come back and visit me." There. He came right out and said it.

A tiny frown appeared between her finely drawn eyebrows. She reached for her glasses and slipped them on to see him better. "What do you mean?"

Crap. This was going to sound really hokey to a woman who, by virtue of her profession, believed in hard, factual evidence. "Ian came to my room the other night. He stood there looking at me while I talked to you on the phone."

He held his breath, waiting for her to say something, but she only blinked, perhaps wondering whether he was pulling her leg.

"He's not the only one. I see them all—every man who's ever died while I was with them. It's not as uncommon as you might think," he added—at least not according to the Edgar Casey Foundation that dealt with the supernatural. He'd visited them on a couple of occasions and found comfort in their assessment that he was perfectly normal.

"Do they . . . um . . . talk to you?" she asked, a thread of reservation woven through her voice.

He couldn't lie. "Sometimes."

Her gaze looked suddenly guarded. "Did Ian talk to you?"

"No. Not yet."

The admission that he fully expected to chat with Ian one day clearly rattled her. She squirmed away from him, signaling her desire for more space.

Damn it. He shifted away, berating himself as she sat up slowly, staring at him like she'd never really seen him before. Something hard and uncomfortable wedged itself beneath his breastbone.

"I guess I shouldn't have told you," he added, as the silence stretched thin between them.

"You're not making this up," she said. The regret in her voice was obvious.

"No." Even to his own ears, his voice sounded weary. Why the fuck would he make up something that made him sound crazy? He'd hoped maybe Ian's spirit had visited her, too, and that she'd understand. But, no. Apparently, only he'd had that dubious honor.

"Okay." She nodded, her gaze sliding toward the fire to gaze at embers. "I need to think about this," she stated in a distant voice.

The ache under his breastbone increased. "Of course."

Just then a loud crack exploded overhead and lightning lit up the beach as bright as day. Darkness followed just as quickly, along with an ominous rumble and a few fat drops of rain.

"I guess we'd better pack up," he said, grateful to the weather for dignifying his retreat by providing an excuse.

What a hell of a way to ruin a perfect evening. Why, oh why, did he have to be so freaking honest?

CURTIS WAITED UNTIL the last echo of the men's footsteps faded. Total darkness pressed in on him, hemming him in like the narrow tunnel he'd been forced to crawl up inside.

They'd searched his pockets for a phone and ended up taking his money. Then they'd swung the tubs full of guns out of the tunnel and forced him to crawl inside, face first.

As he'd craned his neck to look back at them, they closed the grate behind him and replaced the padlock. Then Tom, having dragged a confession out of Santana as to how he'd opened it in the first place, had taken the screwdriver and tamped the screws down tight.

"There's no way he's gettin' out of here now," he'd declared.

They had finally left him there—to die. And not a word or a look from Santana, reassuring him that he would come back for him or call the authorities.

Curtis had watched them walk away, taking the light with them. With the hard plastic of his cell-phone bruising his nuts, he hadn't cried or begged for mercy. He couldn't wait for them to leave.

At last, when all he could hear was the steady trickle of the water chasing through the pipes, he reached inside his drawers and pulled his phone out.

The green glow of the keypad drove back the shadows, staving off his panic. He deliberated a moment—call his mother first or 9-1-1?

He opted for his mom. The phone chirped as he pressed the keys. Then he put it to his ear, breathing heavily as he rehearsed what he was going to say to her.

He waited for a ringing sound . . . and waited . . . and waited.

Oh, no. He glanced at the bars on his screen, and his hopes plummeted. One bar. He didn't have enough cellular reception.

Oh, God, no. He'd been counting on the phone to get him out of there. But the depth of the tunnel and the density of the earth above it kept his phone from working.

Don't panic!

But his lungs labored for oxygen and fear paralyzed him.

No one but Santana and the gun smugglers knew where he was. Santana would be too afraid to tell anyone. He could end up rotting in here, just like Uncle Will had intended!

A sob of fear broke through the stricture of his throat. The cement enclosure magnified the sound, driving home just how terrified he was becoming.

Don't let fear take over. Rusty had never said that to him, but Curtis could practically hear him saying that. What would Rusty do under these circumstances? He'd think his way through it.

He knew the grate was locked. He'd heard the distinct click of the deadbolt after they'd shut him in. Then Tom, having gotten a confession out of Santana that he'd unscrewed the hinges to break in, had taken the screwdriver and twisted the screws down tight. There was no getting out the way Curtis had gone in. So, now what?

A distant rumble of thunder seemed to echo down the pipe he was in. In the next instant an unmistakable wetness touched his elbows, then his belly, then his knees. He lifted himself away from it, only to strike his head and shoulders on the ceiling of the tunnel.

Rainwater.

He snatched up his cell before it got wet and faced its dim light ahead of him. It must be storming outside. Clearly, the tunnel sloped downward if the rain was only now reaching him. That meant if he crawled forward, he'd be headed toward better cellular reception.

Uncle Will had said something about there being no way out. But that couldn't be true if water was coming in. Maybe the line would lead to an opening he could squeeze through. At the very least, he could make a phone call.

Closing his cell with a decisive click, he snuffed out the light. Darkness engulfed him. He slid the phone into his back pocket, swallowed his fear, then started forward. The water that had been seeping down the pipe streamed past his hands and knees, nearly an inch deep. He could hear it pouring out of the drain behind him into the concrete main.

"Oh, come on," he moaned, wondering what would happen if this line continued to fill. What if he drowned down here?

Stay focused.

He crawled as quickly as he could, the rough cement floor abrading his palms and his knees. His breath sawed in the enclosed space, louder even than the sound of water rippling around him.

The tunnel seemed endless. He lost track of how far he'd gone. The water level had crept to his wrists. His palms and knees felt raw. Did this line ever end? He paused for a moment, dried a hand on his T-shirt and pulled out his phone to check for reception. Two bars, yes!

Suddenly something furry bumped into his knee. He jerked reflexively, and tiny claws sank into his thigh.

"Aaagh!" Startled, he shook it off, dropping his phone in the process. It splashed into the water. He groped for it, hoping to snatch it out in time to avoid damage. Where was it? Not there. Not anywhere. The current must have carried it away.

"No!" His howl of despair echoed up and down the tight, dark cylinder.

"Fuck!" he added, because what difference did it make? Thanks to his stupidity and his blind trust, he was stuck in this storm drain. He would either drown in the next few hours, or he'd slowly starve to death. Neither option appealed to him in the least.

"Mom!" He yelled the word that had always brought his mother running.

But the only reply was another distant rumble of thunder. It sounded as far away as it had before he'd started crawling.

With a sob that came from deep down inside of him, Curtis started bawling.

CHAPTER THIRTEEN

MAYA PACED THE length of her bedroom, her bare feet silent on the carpet. Outside her dark window, thunder rumbled, echoing the turmoil in her heart.

Rusty had dropped her off an hour earlier, leaping out of his car to open her door. He'd walked her up her stoop, stopping short of taking her keys to open the lock for her.

A tense silence had enveloped them, making the moment supremely awkward, where she'd hoped it would be silent in an exciting, anticipatory way. If he hadn't brought up that business about ghosts, then she'd have been deliberating whether they would have time before Curtis got home to make love. Instead, all she'd wanted was some time alone, in which to ponder what he'd told her.

Fortunately, he was an astute man. As her door swung open, he'd captured her hand, lifted it to his lips, and softly kissed her knuckles.

"Sleep on it," he'd advised before retreating with the kind of stealth she was coming to associate with him.

But she couldn't sleep. For one thing, Curtis wasn't home yet. She had called him on his cell and texted him, reminding him he was supposed to be home at ten, but his phone went right to voicemail, suggesting his battery had died. She would have to ground him for ignoring his curfew.

Why did children have to test their parents? It only made it harder on the both of them.

Outside thunder gave way to a torrential downpour. Raindrops pelted her windows, filling her with an inexplicable uneasiness. She'd felt the same way when Rusty had mentioned that he saw the dead— he actually *saw* them! How could that be?

As a special investigator, she held great respect for the value of evidence. Evidence was something one could examine, look at, and smell. Where was the proof that ghosts existed, let alone that he could see them? She shook her head while nibbling on a hangnail. It made no sense in her black-and-white take on reality.

Her gaze swung toward Ian's portrait hanging on the wall.

I'm looking at the dead right now, she reasoned. But that was completely different. The picture was solid.

Furthermore, it wasn't Ian looking back at her but merely a likeness of him. And the portrait never talked to her, however much she wished it would.

At least Rusty hadn't asked her to believe him. No, he'd just taken a moment filled with sensual promise and blown it to hell with his, "Oh, by the way, I see dead people."

Had he done it on purpose to derail the moment? Or perhaps he hallucinated due to war injuries or even because of survivor's guilt?

She ought to have known he was too good to be true.

A noose of self-pity closed around her throat. At this rate, she would never love again. Her youth would fade, leaving her a lonely widow for the rest of her days. She supposed she ought to be grateful this had all come about before they'd gotten any closer. For, in her mind, their amazing connection would have taken them swiftly in the direction of marriage.

But now? Probably not.

Her gaze slid to the clock by her bed and worry fell like a rock to the bottom of her belly. Goodness, it was coming up on eleven already! Picking up her phone, she called Curtis again, with the same results.

Had he decided to spend the night with Matt and forgotten to tell her?

Heaving a sigh, she decided to march over to

Matt's house and rouse the family so she could find her son. Her temper simmered. The night she'd looked forward to all week was turning out to be a nightmare.

Raising her eyes to Ian's portrait, she heard herself say, "If you're really there in spirit, then I could use your help right now."

CURTIS EYED THE faint light coming through a hole high above him.

After what felt like hours on his hands and knees, he'd arrived at the end of the line at a catch basin where he could stand up in water that came to his knees. For a heart-stopping moment, he'd thought it was just a dead end and all the crawling had been for nothing.

Patting down the walls, he had felt a concrete ledge and then a rusty bar with another one directly above it—a ladder!

That was when he'd looked up and glimpsed a narrow aperture high above him. Water drizzled through it, but beyond the water, he caught a glimpse of the nighttime sky. A way out!

Sluggish with cold, he climbed awkwardly onto the ledge. Once there, he reached for the rungs of the ladder and stepped carefully onto the algae-slick bar. Hope gave him the impetus to pull his weight upward and climb, one rung at a time toward the suggestion of escape.

Foot by foot, he ascended until he drew eye-level with the opening, several feet wide but only six inches high. Peering through it, he realized that bright new streetlamps were providing the light. He made out a paved road with nothing but trees and stakes in the ground, along with For Sale signs. It struck him as vaguely familiar.

He suddenly realized this was the newest addition to his neighborhood. The road had been paved, but construction had yet to take place. No one ever came here.

He couldn't fit through the intake anyway. It really was a dead end, and he would die here, after all.

About to climb back down, he glimpsed a metallic disk above his head. In the dim light, he made out a manhole cover. There was a way out! Putting a hand flat against it, he pushed up with all his might, fully expecting it to move.

Nope. It didn't shift an inch.

Manhole covers were heavy, but not this heavy.

With panic rising up in him, he shoved upward with everything he had. Suddenly, his footing slipped. He dropped, groping for a rung to catch his descent, but his hand slipped too. With a strangled scream, he fell straight down, striking the ledge with his shoulder.

The *snap* he heard let him know he'd broken something—probably his collarbone. He flipped off the ledge and into water that filled his nose and ears and mouth as he opened it to shout in sudden pain.

In that terrifying moment as he fought his way out of the water so he wouldn't drown, a thought settled in his head like a nail driven into a coffin.

This is where it ends.

THE DOORBELL DIDN'T wake Santana. He was lying in his bed with his eyes wide open when it chimed, sending Lucifer into a barking frenzy in the bedroom behind him. Bolting out of bed, Santana crossed to the window and pressed his cheek to the glass in order to see his front stoop. He both dreaded and hoped that the cops were standing on his dark doorstep.

But it was only Curtis's mother, her golden hair reflecting the street lamp behind her as she stood there wringing her hands, waiting for someone to answer. Guilt plowed into him like a fist to his belly.

What would happen if he threw open the window and called down, *Curtis is trapped in the sewers?*

For one thing, his uncle would kill him. If not his uncle, then his friend Tom would make certain Santana paid the price for telling. If Uncle Will went to jail, who would help Santana's mother pay the rent? Money had been an issue ever since his dad ran off. Uncle Will helped out in his brother's stead, but without *his* help, the collections agents would start calling again like they used to do, all day long. Supposedly, Uncle Will had his shit together, being in the Navy. But that was a lie. Santana knew the real story.

His uncle was a loser just like his father. And Santana wasn't any better than either one of them.

Leaving Curtis in the sewers to die, in the dark and all alone—that made him a murderer.

"I'M SO SORRY to bother you. Are you Santana's mother?" Maya asked as a stranger opened the door.

The haggard, overweight blonde nodded back at her. "Yeah," she admitted on a cautious note. She clutched a robe around her, and clearly had been roused out of bed.

"I'm sorry to intrude so late. I'm Curtis's mother," Maya continued, hoping that the fierce-sounding dog barking in the recesses of the condo was securely restrained. "Has he been by your place at all? He was supposed to be at Matt's this evening, but they said they'd been out for the evening. Did he come here, by any chance?" She didn't care if she was babbling; worry held sway over her tongue.

"Oh." The woman scratched her chin and searched her memory. "No, I haven't seen him tonight."

Maya's dismay deepened. "You haven't seen him," she repeated. Santana's house had been her last option. If Curtis wasn't there, she didn't know where to look. "Could I talk to Santana?" she requested.

The woman at the door seemed to consider her request but then shook her head, no. "He's sleeping," she said on a terse note.

Dark thoughts snaked into Maya's mind, bringing to memory the suspect she was investigating who lived in her neighborhood. Had William Goddard decided to avenge her in advance of his judgment by NCIS? It didn't make sense to avenge someone who hadn't ruined you yet.

She had to be jumping to conclusions.

"Thank you," she mumbled as her brain tried to come up with her next course of action.

"No problem." Santana's mother started closing the door in her face.

At that moment, Maya heard the dog again. Putting out a hand to block the door, she took a shaky breath. "Just curious—is that a Rottweiler you've got in there?" she asked.

"No, it's a Doberman," the woman said, sending her a strange look.

Years of practice kept Maya from displaying the jolt of adrenaline that exploded inside of her. Her intuition had been right. Part of her longed right then to demand to speak to the dog's owner, but she wasn't prepared to confront Will Goddard at that moment—not on her own and not without backup.

"I see. Good night," she said, turning away and hurrying through the drizzle to her condominium.

Practically breaking her own door down as she charged into her condo, she turned, put her shoulder against the paneling, and locked the deadbolt. Her hands shook uncontrollably as she dialed first her colleague at work, explaining to his answering machine what she suspected had happened. Then she called 9-1-1, ordering her thoughts more carefully as the operator answered.

"9-1-1, what's your emergency?"

"This is NCIS Special Investigator, Maya Schultz. I live in Boulevard Crossing. My fourteen-year-old son is missing, and I believe he's been kidnapped by a suspect I'm currently investigating."

"Just a minute, Mrs. Schultz. I'm connecting you with police dispatch."

As Maya's pulse echoed off her eardrums, she suffered an overwhelming urge to call Rusty next. But she couldn't imagine how he could help her or why he would. She'd turned into an ice queen when he'd mentioned ghosts, and he hadn't been able to get away from her condo fast enough. He certainly owed her no assistance.

Besides, she'd been dealing with every crisis by herself for a decade. And she would do the same thing tonight.

"Police dispatch. What's your emergency?"

It took ten nerve-fraying minutes to persuade the police to put a BOLO out on Curtis. Because he wasn't a three-year-old but a male teenager, they weren't convinced he was really missing but, rather, acting out. It took a threat to involve the FBI before they agreed to send two officers to her home immediately.

Wishing she could turn to Rusty for solace, Maya put her phone away and fetched her laptop, settling in to do some research of her own. There just might be something in William Goddard's file that would suggest why and where he would have taken Curtis.

RUSTY JERKED AWAKE, and Draco leaped from the bed as if it were exploding.

"Sorry, buddy, sorry," he crooned as the dog fought to get inside the closet.

Swinging his feet to the floor, Rusty continued to croon comforting words while reconsidering the dream that had awakened him.

Ian had been crouched next to him, firing away on the M240. The clatter of the grenade rolling toward them had grown louder. Rusty knew what would happen next. He'd dreamed it so often that he knew every detail of the dream right down to the feel of grit between his teeth. But this time, Ian didn't just look down at the grenade and then at him with that look of absolute resolve. This time he spoke.

"My son needs help." And then he dove face-down on top of the grenade and it blew up under him, waking Rusty up.

"Curtis needs help," he repeated to the dog, who licked his hand.

Were the words real or just a spin-off of a recurring nightmare? With his heart still thudding in his chest, Rusty snatched his phone off the bedside table. Maya hadn't texted him. There was nothing going on with Curtis; it was all in his head.

Except he couldn't shake the certainty that Ian had just spoken from the other side.

What to do? Call Maya to ask if Curtis was okay? He dismissed the idea. She already thought him a lunatic for claiming to see ghosts. He looked at Draco who sat there regarding him expectantly. He had to do something. He would head over to her place and at least take a look. If Curtis really was in trouble, then there ought to be some sign. He'd be better off shooting himself in the foot than waking Maya up for no reason.

She wasn't going to have anything to do with

him if she thought he'd become delusional.

"MA'AM—" THE OLDER officer who stood at her breakfast bar scanning the file on William Godfrey shook his head, "I hear what you're saying, but there's not enough evidence to suggest an abduction. Do you have any witnesses?"

He'd already asked her that question. "No."

"Any evidence besides a barking dog?"

"No." She paused, fighting the panic clawing inside her to remain rational in front of these officers. "All the evidence I have is that my son is still missing."

"But Goddard has no motive for revenge since NCIS hasn't yet prosecuted."

"Yes, he does. His pay has been reduced. He'll probably get passed over for an upcoming promotion since he's under investigation. You should have seen the look he gave me when he realized who I was. My son goes over to his house all the time to hang out with his son or his nephew—I don't know what their relationship is. Can't you at least question him?"

"We can knock on his door and talk to him if he answers," the officer offered.

"Please," she begged.

He heaved a sigh of annoyance while meeting

the other officer's eyes. It was clear they both thought Curtis was fine. Boys his age disappeared all the time. He'd be back in the morning.

"As long as you keep your distance," he replied. "Hurling accusations at the man isn't going to help anything."

"Of course," she agreed.

Slapping his hat onto his balding head, Officer Ramsey headed for her exit with his colleague. Maya chased them to the door. They had parked their cruisers in the middle of the complex. The sirens were silent, but their blue lights strobed the brick facades of the condominiums around her. She could see the faces of several neighbors peeking out of adjacent windows.

Too distraught to care, she planted herself on her front stoop and watched the officers make their way up the road to Santana's condo. His mother wouldn't be happy to see them, Maya was sure. But it was William Goddard they wanted to talk to.

It had stopped raining, she noted absently. Heat rose off the pavement, forming an eerie mist in the cooler air. Crickets and tree frogs played background music as Ramsey and his colleague, Officer Reynolds, climbed the stairs to knock at Santana's front door.

Maya clutched the wrought iron railing until her knuckles ached. In her peripheral vision she noted and dismissed a vehicle approaching from the other direction. It swerved into a parking space one door down from hers.

Her gaze was glued to the officers as one of them raised a hand to knock.

The loud bark of a dog yanked her attention to the car that had just arrived. As Rusty leaped out of the driver's side door, Maya glimpsed Draco's snout jutting out of the lowered back window.

The wave of relief that swamped her as Rusty stepped up alongside her caught her completely off guard. She hadn't realized until that moment how much stress she'd been holding in for so many hours.

"Rusty!" His unexpected appearance ripped away her self-control, causing her to burst into embarrassing sobs as she turned to greet him.

"Hey." He swept her against him without an ounce of hesitation, holding her upright as she sagged against him, suddenly exhausted. "What happened?"

"It's Curtis," she managed to choke between convulsions of her lungs. She forced herself to loosen her fierce hold. "He's missing," she added, dashing the wetness from her cheeks.

He nodded, looking not the least surprised to hear it.

She turned in his arms to point out the officers

standing at Santana's door. "They're going to question William Goddard. He's under investigation by NCIS—one of my cases, actually—for suspicion of theft. A shipment of weapons went missing under his watch—him and two others. I didn't realize it, but the boy who lives with him is Curtis's friend, Santana."

Rusty stiffened as he followed her gaze. "No one's answering," he stated.

Sure enough, Ramsey and Reynolds were coming off the stoop and heading back in her direction.

"No," she moaned. She already knew what this meant. They couldn't force William Goddard to speak to them—not without a warrant, which no judge would issue at this time of night—let alone ever—given the scarcity of evidence.

Draco suddenly issued a rash of fierce barks that raised the hair on Maya's nape. The officers hesitated, leery of coming any closer.

"Sorry," Rusty said out the side of his mouth. "He sleeps with me. I was afraid he'd destroy my room if I left him behind."

"Let him out," Maya suggested.

"You sure?" He seemed hesitant to impose.

The dog reminded her of Curtis. "Yes. Let him out."

As Rusty went to get Draco from the car, Ramsey and Reynolds made their way closer.

"No one's answering, ma'am." Ramsey kept a wary eye on Draco while planting his right hand on his hip, close to his gun. "The most we can do is park at the entrance to your neighborhood and see if he leaves. Sometimes perps get leery and make a run for it. If he does, we'll pull him over on a traffic citation and have a word with him then."

Maya's throat constricted. That was it? That was all they could do to help? Curtis was in trouble. He needed help *now*.

Draco stopped barking as Rusty released him from the car. He strained at the leash Rusty held, scrabbling onto her stoop to sniff at Maya's shorts. His tail began to wag.

"Is that a working dog?" Officer Reynolds asked, staring intently at Draco.

"He's a retired MWD."

"Gorgeous animal. I used to work with a K-9. Too bad he can't find your boy for you."

Maya looked over at him sharply.

"We'll be in touch, ma'am." Ramsey tipped his hat to her, and the two men turned away, heading to their respective vehicles.

Too stricken to speak, Maya watched them drive away. They hadn't done a blessed thing to help her. As their taillights blinked out of sight, Rusty put a warm hand on her back.

"Why don't we take Draco for a walk?" he suggested.

The unexpected offer had her instantly pinning her hopes on the dog. It must have shown on her face for Rusty gave a slight shake of his head.

"I'm sorry. Draco was trained to find firearms and explosives, not people—unless, of course, they're carrying weapons."

She wanted to scream with frustration, but once again, she kept calm in the face of the helpless and terrified voice in her mind urging her to lose control. True, she had hit a mental wall more than once over the past few hours, but she kept reminding herself that she was all Curtis had to count on. She could not let him down.

"Draco looks too keyed up to go inside anyway," she said quietly, "so . . . maybe we could just try. After all, he knows Curtis."

"I just don't want you to expect a miracle from this dog," Rusty said.

"I won't," she promised, "but let me grab one of Curtis's T-shirts or his jacket so Draco knows who we're looking for."

"Maya—" Rusty began.

"Just in case," she said. In a flash, she had entered her condo and returned with one of Curtis's well-worn shirts. Before Rusty could stop her, she bent down and waved it in front of the dog, then rubbed it on the end of his nose, with no idea if she was doing it correctly. The dog showed a brief momentary interest, then turned away.

What had she expected? That Draco would become the famed Lassie and start leading them immediately to her son? Instead, they ambled along, walking the dog in the opposite direction from William Goddard's condo.

Numb with exhaustion and hopelessness, Maya tagged along, scarcely registering the sweet scent of freshly washed grass or the cool air that swirled around her bare legs as Rusty let out Draco's lead. The Malinois loped ahead of them in an S-pattern, doing what he'd been trained to do without being asked.

When Rusty reached out and caught Maya's hand, a question seized her simultaneously.

How had he known that she needed him?

Draco gave a sudden jerk on the leash, pulling them off the sidewalk to the opposite side of the street. Maya took advantage of the approaching street lamp to search Rusty's profile.

Like the dog, he appeared fully alert, his senses receptive to the environment. SEALs were famous for heeding their intuition, but how could Rusty have known anything was amiss? Or had he come over for some other reason?

She slowed to a stop, causing their hands to fall apart as the dog continued to propel Rusty forward.

"Draco, *zit*." The dog immediately sat, and Rusty swung back around to look at her, a questioning look on his face.

"Why are you here, Rusty?" she demanded.

Her traumatized mind wondered if he and Curtis hadn't set this scenario up together—some sort of bizarre plot to win her over. Curtis could be waiting somewhere, unharmed, certain Rusty would lead her straight to him, thereby proving himself a hero of the highest caliber.

Rusty just looked at her. The longer his compassionate gaze rested on her, the less she believed he would conspire with Curtis in order to win her over. Besides, Curtis had only just learned that his mother and the SEAL had in interest in each other. Why would he want to make Rusty look good?

"You asked me earlier tonight if Ian ever spoke to me," Rusty said.

It took her a second to realize he was answering her question.

A chill settled over her, causing the hair on the back of her neck to rise. What did Ian have to do with any of this?

"He did, earlier tonight," Rusty continued.

The chill glided over her shoulders and down her arms, sprouting goosebumps. "What did he say?" she whispered.

"That Curtis needed help."

The breath in Maya's lungs congealed. She could tell by the gravely monotone in which Rusty spoke that he wasn't inventing tales. She didn't believe in ghosts—at least, she *hadn't*—but fear still whipped her heart into a gallop. After all, the evidence that Rusty spoke the truth was the fact that he was standing in front of her and her son was missing.

"We have to find him," she said in a strangled voice.

Reaching for her, Rusty caught up her hand again, offering his strength. He didn't make an outlandish promise that they would find Curtis, but as he squeezed her hand in his, she felt that together, they could.

"Draco, *zoek*," Rusty said quietly.

The dog took off again, pulling them between the parked cars that faced the sidewalk. The dog might not be trained to find people, but Draco tested the air, put his nose to the concrete, then jerked them back in the direction of Santana's home.

Maya's hopes fluttered. "I think he smells something."

"Maybe," Rusty allowed.

CHAPTER FOURTEEN

M AYA'S HAND FELT like ice in Rusty's grasp, conveying the depths of her fear. Christ, she didn't deserve this—not after what she'd suffered losing her husband.

Perhaps he was grasping at straws, but Draco definitely was behaving as if he was scenting a target. He strained toward William Goddard's condo, his hackles bristling, his ears swiveling like satellite dishes on the top of his head.

Did Draco think, in his warped, post-traumatic canine mind that he was back in Afghanistan, hunting down ISIS sympathizers? How could his behavior have anything to do with Curtis's disappearance? And yet—

A shadow drifting through the green space up ahead prompted Rusty to hustle Maya off the sidewalk in between a parked motorcycle and a conversion van. Reeling a resisting Draco in after them, he peered over the van's hood as the silhouette of a man rounded the front corner of Goddard's end unit.

Maya peeked over his shoulder. "It's Will Goddard," she whispered.

As Draco started to growl, Rusty dropped into a crouch banding a hand around the dog's muzzle to silence him.

Draco submitted to his hold, but the growl still rumbled in his chest.

The bark of a second dog supplied the reason for Draco's aggression.

"Shut up, Lucifer," muttered Will Goddard.

Several options raced through Rusty's mind as he tightened his grip on Draco's collar. He could free the dog with the order to "*reveire.*" If Goddard had a weapon, Draco would attack him, hampering his departure. But then he'd have to deal with Goddard's dog, not to mention a chance that the man would shoot the MWD. And Maya herself might come to harm if Goddard caught sight of her.

"Where might you be going?"

The sound of her voice, forceful and full of accusation, caught Rusty completely off guard. He straightened, realizing she had rounded the back of the van to intercept Goddard's departure.

"Where's my son?" she demanded, blocking Goddard's access to his vehicle.

Her ambush had startled Goddard back onto his lawn. For a moment, it looked like he would bolt for the woods behind the condos. But then, seeing she was all alone, he lifted his chin and held his ground.

"Whatchu talkin' about, woman?" he scoffed. "I don't know your son."

"Yes, you do. He plays video games with Santana."

Maya sounded angry enough to attack the man physically. As she stepped off the sidewalk onto his lawn, he reached behind his back, no doubt intending to retrieve a hidden weapon. Rusty didn't wait to find out.

"*Reveire*," he hissed unhooking Draco's lead. At the same time, he withdrew his Gerber blade from beneath his pant leg.

Like a black phantom, Draco streaked out of his hiding place. The Doberman noticed him first, careening into his owner as he pranced sideways.

William looked up. "What the—?"

Hurdling the Doberman, Draco struck Goddard with paws outstretched. The man went down, screaming as Draco landed on top of him, sinking his teeth into his shoulder.

The Doberman defended his master and lit into Draco, who leaped off of Goddard to face his challenger. To the sound of snapping jaws and blood-curdling snarls, Rusty sprinted over to Maya, and pushed her in the direction of the parked cars with an order to call the cops. He kept an eye pinned on Goddard, who sat up clutching his shoulder with one hand, a pistol with the other. The whites of his eyes shone up at Rusty as he raised a nine millimeter with a shaky hand.

Rusty let him see the Gerber blade, which he could throw as fast as the man could fire at him. "You don't want to shoot me," he said on a certain note.

One of the dogs gave a yelp of pain.

"Draco, *los!*" Rusty commanded, certain it wasn't his dog who'd gotten hurt. "*Los!*" he repeated and Draco released his opponent, which darted behind its master and cowered there.

Rusty reached for Draco's collar. The ex-military dog growled at Goddard, eying him intently. The man aimed his weapon at Draco.

"I wouldn't do that," Rusty cautioned. "One bullet isn't going to stop him. Go ahead and put your gun down. The police are on their way anyway." At least, he hoped Maya had called them.

Goddard kept his pistol trained on the dog. Tensing, Rusty prepared to hurl his dagger before the man got a shot off. But then, with a sigh of defeat, Goddard lowered his weapon and laid it on the grass.

"Hands in the air," Rusty suggested, hearing the

sirens approaching a moment before glimpsing blue lights heading in their direction. "Don't move," he added, slipping his own weapon back into the strap at his ankle.

As the cruisers screeched to a stop in front of the condo, Maya greeted them with a quick explanation. Ramsey and Reynolds approached Goddard with their weapons drawn. But Goddard was clutching his shoulder, apparently in too much pain to resist arrest.

Now the police could question him. Soon, they might have answers as to where they could find Curtis—assuming this creep had made the boy disappear.

Please, oh, please, Rusty thought, *don't let this man have murdered Maya's son.*

SANTANA JIMMIED OPEN his bedroom window, got on his knees, and pressed his ear to the screen to listen.

"—ain't got nuthin' to do with that," he heard his uncle insist.

Why hadn't the cops arrested him? They'd taken his gun, but they were letting him just stand there talking shit while Curtis's mother stood gnawing on her fingernails, in the embrace of that stranger with the dog. And all this time Curtis was buried underground . . . probably freakin' out.

"Then why were you running off just now?" one of the officers demanded. "What have you got to hide?"

"Man, I don't need this harassment. You chargin' me with something or not?"

Uncle Will had some nerve talking to the cops like he was all innocent. Santana licked his dry lips, tempted to say something.

"We'll start with you carrying a concealed weapon," one of the officers suggested.

"I got a right to defend myself," his uncle retorted. "This crazy woman verbally assaulted me, and then *his* dog attacked me, and he threatened to knife me."

"Don't pretend you don't recognize me, Seaman Goddard," Curtis's mother spoke up.

"Where is Curtis Schultz?" a cop asked.

Santana swallowed hard.

"Who?"

"This woman's son."

"How should I know?"

His uncle wasn't going to tell them. The pressure that was just starting to ease off Santana's chest returned, making it hard to breathe. Curtis was going to die, making Santana an accessory to murder.

Tell them, said a voice inside his head.

His stomach churned. He couldn't. Uncle Will would hear him, and then he'd kill him or send someone to do it.

Just then Santana's mother stepped out of their front door.

"Listen here," she spoke up on a harried note, "I got to go to work tomorrow, and all this nonsense is keeping me awake. I don't need you bringing trouble to my door, William. I had enough trouble with your brother. Get your stuff and get out of here."

Her words gave Santana the impetus to speak up. "I know where Curtis is," he blurted. Six sets of eyes swiveled toward his second-story window.

"Don't you say nothin', boy," Uncle Will warned, his dark eyes glinting.

"Where is Curtis, Santana?" Mrs. Schultz cried, crossing the lawn to stand directly below his window. She gazed up at him beseechingly. "Tell me," she added on a note that would break anyone's heart.

Uncle William pointed a warning finger at him. In the dark it looked like a gun.

Santana's mother stormed off the front steps. "Don't you threaten my son, Will," she warned flying toward him.

He put both hands into the air and backed away. "That's it. I don't need this shit."

"Where are you going?" a cop asked him.

"Santana, please!" Mrs. Schultz cried.

His mother looked at her then up at Santana's

window. "What does she want?" she demanded.

Uncle Will ignored the policemen and stalked doggedly toward his car, taking Lucifer with him. Blood streamed from his shoulder and down his arm, but he didn't seem to notice.

"Stay right there, Goddard." One of the officers pointed his gun at Uncle Will's back.

"You ain't got no reason to arrest me," Will said, without turning around. Opening the driver's door on his Oldsmobile, he ordered his dog inside before ducking in behind him.

"Yes, he does," Santana said, but not so loud that Will could hear him.

"Santana! Where is Curtis?" Mrs. Schultz cried in an anxious voice.

Santana waited until his uncle turned the engine over and was backing out of his parking place. As he drove away, he looked down at Curtis's mother's pale face and said with a tremendous sense of relief, "Uncle Will locked him in the sewers in the woods behind us. That's where he's been hiding the guns that him and his friends stole."

The two police officers whipped their attention to Uncle Will's departing vehicle. "We'll send officers to help look for your son," one of them promised as they sprinted for their cruisers. Apparently, the boy's confession gave them all the testimony they needed to arrest Uncle Will without a warrant.

As they departed with their sirens screaming, the lights in several neighboring condos blinked on.

Mrs. Schultz stood below him with her hands on her cheeks, her eyes enormous eyes. "Can you show us where to look?" she asked.

Santana glanced at his mother who stood next to Curtis's mother with her hand on her hips and her mouth hanging open. "Boy, you better fix this now," his mother warned.

"Yeah," he said to Mrs. Schultz. "I'll be right down."

CHAPTER FIFTEEN

"IT'S DOWN THIS way."

Santana's quavering voice echoed in the dank catchment basin he had led them into moments earlier. Maya fought to keep her horror at bay as she, Rusty, and Draco followed a hesitant Santana deeper and deeper into the trunk line, while Santana's mother remained outside with a promise to send the police after them.

Cold rainwater sluiced past Maya's calves, carrying all sorts of unidentified debris that brushed her bare legs. She scarcely noticed. Rusty's warm fingers clasping hers steadied her resolve, unlike poor Santana, who shivered so violently that the light cast by his penlight jerked violently on the walls. Pulling out her cellphone, she contributed to the feeble lighting with its flashlight feature. Its bright white light made the six-foot tunnel seem less daunting.

But the farther into the tunnel they walked, the

more apprehensive she became. When they came upon an intersection suggesting a maze of underground tunnels, her dismay mounted.

"How much farther?" she asked.

"Almost there," Santana promised.

She called her son's name, straining her ears for a reply, but all she heard was the steady rush of water and the echo of her own voice.

Santana had begun to pan the walls with his light. When it rested on a bolted grate through which water poured, her heart stopped and then beat double-time. She stared at the thick padlock, realizing at once that it didn't belong there.

"This is where they hid the guns," Santana said, his voice displaying the terror she was feeling. "But Tom took them somewhere else after we found them."

Bending over the grate, the boy shone his light into the lateral line on the other side. "Curtis!" he shouted, his voice on the verge of a sob.

Maya added her light to his, trying to see inside the dark tube, but Draco's head blocked her view as he pushed his way forward to sniff at the grate.

"He smells the residual gunpowder from the rifles," Rusty explained.

"How do we get it open?" Maya asked.

Santana produced a screwdriver. Applying it to one of the hinges, he grimaced as he fought to turn it.

"Where's Curtis now?" Maya asked, alarmed by the quantity of water gushing out of the grate to spill into the bigger channel. "You said he was here, right?"

Santana cast her a frightened glance. "Maybe he tried crawling out the other way."

"Where does it lead?" she asked.

"I don't know. My uncle said there's no way out."

Her heart thudded painfully at his ominous words. Obviously, if there'd been a way out of his dark watery prison, Curtis would have returned home.

"Here, let me try that, son." Taking over the screwdriver, Rusty used his superior strength to turn the screws on both hinges. He spun them out of their threads, tugged the grate from the hole, and something fell out as he did, splashing into the stream at her feet.

Maya bent down to retrieve the object. "It's Curtis's cellphone. Curtis!" she cried, angling her light into the dark conduit. She repeated his name, but there was nothing to be seen or heard, merely an empty offshoot filled with rushing water. At ten yards or so, it angled upward and her light went no farther.

To everyone's astonishment, Draco leapt suddenly into the opening, crawled forward, and disappeared.

At the other end of his lead, Rusty tried to follow, but his shoulders scraped the cement walls on either side, hampering his advancement. He wriggled back out, the front of his T-shirt soaked, his hands empty.

He'd let Draco proceed without him.

"I'll go," Maya volunteered, uncertain how to hold her iPhone while scrambling after the dog.

Rusty stopped her. "It's not safe, Maya. Let the dog go. We need to find the intake that this line comes from." He held up his left wrist on which he wore a thick tactical watch, angling it in the direction Draco had taken. "This line is headed northwest."

"But one of us should stay here." She wouldn't leave in case Curtis could hear them all abandoning him.

"I'll stay," Santana said, his eyes bright with tears. "It's my fault this happened. I'll stay right here in case the dog comes back with Curtis."

Rusty laid a hand on his shoulder. "We'll send in an officer or two to keep you company," he reassured the teen. "Come on, Maya. We need to do this quickly."

His urgency alarmed her. Clearly, the situation was a dire one. The water pouring out of the conduit was cool. If Curtis was caught somewhere in the lead between the main and the catch basin, he could drown or succumb to hypothermia, or both.

Following immediately behind the focused SEAL, she created a wake in the shallow water in her haste to exit the underground maze.

CURTIS SURFACED TO awareness as a moist snout snuffled his forearm, then his shoulder, and then his face.

What the hell?

With a yelp of alarm, and envisioning some kind of oversized sewer rat, he cringed, while trying to thrust the creature away from the ledge he lay on. Pain immediately tore through his left side, but it waned when the animal returned, licking his forearm in a friendly manner and bumping his hand with its head.

Amazement broke over Curtis, sharpening his awareness as, unmistakably, a dog bounded onto the ledge and stood over him, panting hot breath onto his face.

"Draco?" he cried, recognizing the texture of the animal's fur and the shape of his body.

A sob of relief escaped him at the realization he'd been found. He wasn't going to die here, after all. Seizing Draco's collar, he discovered the length of his lead still attached to it. Where was Rusty who no doubt had held the other end?

"Rusty!" Curtis tried shouting, but his voice was feeble and too hoarse from crying out earlier to carry very far.

He collapsed back against the ledge, clinging tightly to the dog, and keeping him from bumping his left shoulder. The SEAL couldn't come the way the dog had, but he was nearby, looking for him. Of that, Curtis was certain.

"Draco, you found me." Curtis's cold lips were scarcely able to form words.

The dog started to pull away.

"No!" Curtis tightened his hold on the collar. "*Blijf,*" he ordered. Stay.

Left any longer by himself, he knew he would succumb to hypothermia, as soaked as he was. "*Af,*" he added, commanding the dog to lie down. As Draco stretched out next to him, Curtis pulled him closer, huddling against the merciful heat radiating off the dog's body.

Succumbing to his exhaustion, he closed his eyes with the expectation of being saved soon.

RUSTY DIDN'T WAIT for the police to come up with blueprints from the land developer that had mapped the storm drainage system. Sending a couple of officers into the main to join Santana, he'd produced paper and pen from the glove box of his car. Then he'd stood over the hood mapping the tunnel himself, adding angles, approximating distance and direction to determine, if possible, where the lead came out at street level.

Maya watched him work with her heart in her throat. Was it fair of her to expect him to save her son? Because that's exactly what she was doing, depending on this man who had no responsibility to help, yet knowing he would do absolutely everything he could for her and for Curtis.

"This way," he said, stuffing the paper into his pocket and grabbing Maya's hand. He tugged her up the street toward the back of the neighborhood.

The remaining officers, like the dozens of SEALs he'd led over the course of his career, responded automatically to his authority and fell in behind them. They all passed Santana's house, now lit up like a Christmas tree. Maya hadn't heard whether William Goddard had been apprehended, but she no longer cared enough to spare a thought for him.

"Nothing's been built back here yet," she stated as Rusty turned toward the newly paved street leading to the latest phase of construction in her neighborhood.

He pointed to the recently poured sidewalks. "But the drainage system is in place."

Coming upon a storm drain in the gutter, Rusty

dropped into a prone position with his face next to the opening and whistled for Draco.

But the only sound to reach their ears was the intermittent peeping of tree frogs and the ever-present sound of running water. Rusty pushed to his feet and they continued down the road to the next curbside drain where he repeated his efforts. This time, a bark came from somewhere farther up the road.

"It's the next one!" Rusty leaped to his feet and ran another fifty yards to crouch beside the next gutter. As he whistled again, the dog's eager barks echoed in the catch basin below him.

Catching up to Rusty, Maya dropped to her knees beside him.

"Curtis, are you down there?"

"Mom!" came his voice back to her, the most blessed sound she'd ever heard. Relief all but flattened her. He was alive!

"Are you hurt, honey?" She held her breath waiting for a report.

"Broke my…collar bone, I think."

"Hold on, baby. We'll have you out in a minute."

But she could see that the slotted gutter was too narrow to fit through. Beside her, Rusty had spied a manhole cover on the curb and was straining to lift it. Strangely, it didn't budge, even while his biceps bulged with his effort.

He gave up with a frustrated roar and rose to his feet. "It's cemented down or something."

He focused his attention on the officers who formed a semi-circle around them. "We're going to need a jackhammer with a chisel tip."

Responding to the command in Rusty's voice, an officer was on his phone in two seconds flat.

Heedless of the damp pavement, Maya sprawled in front of the slotted inlet so she could shine her light into the well and see her son. Draco's eyes, glowing gold, were the first thing she noticed as the dog glanced up at her before resting its head back down. Then she made out Curtis lying next to him, holding onto the dog like a lifeline, and something in her heart shifted.

She angled the light so she could take in Curtis's pale face, his pursed, blue lips testifying as to how chilled he was and in how much pain. He flinched from the light, then looked back at her.

Maya's throat closed up. Lying that way, her growing boy struck her as utterly helpless. Injured as he was, he wouldn't have been able to climb toward the high opening to call for help. Crawling back the way he'd come wouldn't have helped him either. He would have died there if not for Draco.

The dog had saved his life.

"I'm right here with you, honey," she said, all but sobbing with the need to hold her boy. "It's going to take a little time to find the right tool, but you'll be out really soon."

"I'm okay, Mom," he said, sounding stronger in answer to the wobble in her voice.

"Yes, you are. You're just fine."

CHAPTER SIXTEEN

A T SIX O'CLOCK in the morning, with a bright
sun already scaling the face of her condo,
Maya and Rusty climbed the stoop to her front
door, while Draco watched them from the back
window of Rusty's car. They'd left Curtis sleeping
peacefully in a hospital room where he would be
monitored for another twenty-four hours. His
collarbone had been set, and his arm put in a sling.
Given his excellent prognosis, the nurses on staff
had suggested Maya get some sleep herself, so Rusty
had driven her home.

She assumed he would want to get back to his
retreat and his many guests, but as she reached for
her keys, he stood there, watching her every move,
appearing to be waiting. She was reminded of the
end of their date—good God, was it only the previous night? It seemed as if it had been a lifetime ago.
But, yes, only last night he'd murmured goodbye and

walked away.

Her pulse quickened when it occurred to her that he might kiss her this time.

And why stop there? She'd realized over the course of the night that she both needed and wanted Rusty in her life, permanently. It was time to show him, not with words but with actions, that she accepted him, visitations from the dead and all.

Inserting her key into the lock, she lifted her gaze to his as she opened her front door. "Why don't you fetch Draco and come in, the two of you? There's no reason why you can't . . . rest here."

One dark auburn eyebrow rose higher than the other. "The dog, too?"

"You're a package deal, aren't you?" She glanced over at Draco's muzzle now sticking out of the cracked window. "Besides, I love that dog."

"You *love* him," Rusty repeated. His eyes took on a distinct twinkle.

"He saved Curtis's life last night," she continued. "And so did you," she added, holding his gaze to convey the depth of her gratitude.

"So, if the dog gets your love," Rusty reasoned in a careful voice, "what do I get?"

She noted his expanded chest. "Are you holding your breath?"

"Yes." He nodded several times. The eager look on his face made her throw her head back and laugh.

God, that felt good! Throwing her arms around him, she demonstrated just how much he'd get by crushing her lips to his.

As he locked her in a possessive embrace, exhilaration soared through her, heightening the sensual pleasure of their mouths fusing. In mere seconds, their kiss morphed into a deep, passionate exchange of longing and need.

But they couldn't undress each other on her front stoop. Maya pulled reluctantly away and assessed him carefully. She still didn't know what his intentions were.

"Curtis and I are a package deal, too," she said. "I need to know if you intend a long-term arrangement, or if I'm just a passing interest to you."

His expression became incredulous. "Do I strike you as a player?"

The descriptor couldn't be more inaccurate. She laughed, then responded with a resounding, "No."

He sighed and took her hands. "I never married when I was a SEAL because I didn't think it was fair to a woman to ask her to give everything to a man who might not come back to her."

His reference to marriage sobered her immediately. She swallowed hard and listened.

"But I'm retired now."

It hadn't occurred to her that he might have been waiting to marry and start a family of his own, but it did so suddenly. What if—

"If you want a family," she said, shaking her head regretfully, "Curtis is my one and only. I had to have a hysterectomy years ago."

He squeezed her hands. "I'm sorry."

His compassion made her realize she'd never grieved the potential loss of future children. She'd merely accepted it and moved on.

"That makes no difference to me," he assured her. "I have my hands full with the retreat. And if Curtis is okay with having me for a stepdad, I'd be proud to call him my son."

Tears flooded Maya's eyes. "I can't imagine he'd complain. But right now, I think we're both a little punch-drunk from lack of sleep. It's probably not the best time to plan our entire future together."

Rusty frowned, probably thinking she was giving him the brush-off. Quickly, she added, "So get the dog and come on in."

THIRTY MINUTES LATER, with dirty breakfast dishes left by the sink and Draco stretched out on the kitchen floor, his belly distended with eggs and sausages, Maya offered Rusty the use of the bath-room upstairs, then disappeared into her bedroom. He noted that she left her door ajar as she shut herself into her *en suite*.

Once in Curtis's bathroom, Rusty regarded the

face in the mirror and marveled that he didn't look like a man who'd been up all night. Yes, there was a trace of bristles on his jaw and his auburn hair stood up in places. But his face shone with a radiance he hadn't seen—or felt—in years. Maya had practically agreed to marry him!

He grinned sheepishly as he stripped off his clothes to wash up. Whether they slept together that morning or not, he still smelled like the manhole that he had climbed out of carrying a grim-faced Curtis over his shoulder. That had been no easy feat for either one of them, but Rusty was used to dragging around wounded men almost twice his size. And Curtis had shown remarkable composure and bravery considering how much pain he was in.

Taking a quick hot shower, Rusty wondered as he soaped up whether his compact, muscle-corded physique would live up to Maya's expectations. And then he dismissed his worry. He wasn't Ian, but she already knew that and seemed to like who he was just fine.

When he descended the steps a short while later, Maya's open bedroom door caused him to drift toward the soft scent emanating from within. Intent on the woman waiting for him, he barely registered the décor except to note its understated elegance. Given her decorating taste, she would like his bedroom, too. How long before she'd be willing to share it with him on a nightly basis and let him wake up next to her every morning?

Wondering whether to sit on her bed or tap on her bathroom door, Rusty was crossing the room when his gaze glanced off and then returned to an oil portrait that occupied a prime position. Halting in front of it, he tried to decide if it captured the true essence of Ian Schultz. Suddenly, the door to Maya's *en suite* opened, and she emerged, wresting his attention to her petite figure adorned by a gold, satin teddy with possibly nothing underneath. His mouth went dry.

"Will that bother you?" she asked, having caught him looking at the portrait.

Her comment sent his blood pressure spiking. She *was* going to sleep with him for sure.

He couldn't stop staring. Wearing no makeup, with her tumble of golden curls and her pale, soft-looking skin, she resembled an angel. He swallowed hard to find his voice.

"Doesn't bother me. Ian already gave me his blessing."

"Oh?" Her smile struck him as skeptical. "What did he say?"

Rusty had trouble remembering with the tips of Maya's breasts visible through the sheer fabric of her teddy.

"Well, nothing, actually. I asked if he minded me

asking you out. He shook his head. Then I asked if he thought I could win you over, and he smiled like he knew something I didn't."

Maya's smile faded. "My God," she said.

His stomach clenched. "What?" Had he said something wrong?

"That's exactly how Ian communicated. He never talked if he could get his point across with a smile or a frown or a gesture."

Rusty didn't want to talk about Ian.

He took two steps in her direction. "I'd like to make a few points with body language," he proposed. "Do you think I can get my message across that way?" he asked, trailing the tips of his fingers from her wrists to her shoulders.

"I'm sure you can," she said, in a breathier voice. "But I don't mind if you also want to use words."

"Good," he said cupping her face with his hands, "because I have something to tell you." He brushed the pad of one thumb lightly over her lower lip, watching as her pupils dilated.

"What?"

"I love you," he stated. He had thought the confession might be difficult but it flowed from him with the ease of water flowing downstream.

Her lovely green eyes grew brighter, and a tremulous smile curled the edges of her mouth.

"I think I fell in love with you last year when I

came to your office. I'd never met a woman as strong and beautiful as you are. But you didn't like me much," he recalled.

"On the contrary." Tears of joy now welled in her eyes. "I liked you too much, and it frightened me."

"Are you still afraid?" Lowering one hand, he traced the slope of her shoulder to the swell of one breast and lightly outlined her nipple with his index finger, causing it to harden instantly.

"Not at all," she told him.

"Do you think I'm crazy for seeing ghosts?"

Her tiny frown conveyed puzzlement, and his worries returned. But then she shook her head.

"There's obviously something to that," she said, measuring her words with care, "something I don't understand. All I know is if Ian hadn't talked to you last night, you and Draco would never have come back here, and Curtis would still be stuck down in that sewer hurt and freezing to death." She shuddered at the memory of how helpless he'd looked.

"He's safe," Rusty reminded her, slipping his hands to her tiny waist and tugging her close.

She nodded, visibly shaking off the recollection. Then, with a look of lusty resolve, she slid her arms around his neck and pressed her mouth to his, bestowing on him a kiss—the sweetest and sexiest kiss of invitation imaginable.

"I love you, too," she murmured against his lips. To his surprise, he felt her hands slide to the fly of his khaki pants, which he'd been loath to put back on after his shower, stained as they were from their trek through the storm drain. "Take these off," she ordered.

He obeyed her eagerly, shucking off the dirty pants while leaving his boxer briefs on—not that they disguised his eagerness to be with her. Pausing only to close the door between them and his dog, he pulled her modest curves close once more, basking in the feel of her pliant softness pressed so trustingly against him.

They kissed until the room seemed to spin in a lazy circle. Then he lifted her off her feet, keeping their lips fused as he deposited her gently on the bed. Tearing his lips from hers, he stretched out alongside Maya, looking down at her lovely face with wonder.

What had he done to deserve this moment? He didn't know, but this was undoubtedly one of the highlights of his arduous life.

She reached up and touched his cheek, and silently, he pledged to give her everything he had, to make her happy, to make up for the years of her loneliness, to be the only man she would want for the rest of her life.

Nuzzling the length of her neck, Rusty took his

time as he kissed the soft slope of her shoulders, the fragrant plane between her breasts, and then grazed his teeth lightly over each erect peak jutting against the fabric of her satin lingerie.

Her breath hitched, and her spine arched at his ministrations. Glancing at her face, he intended this to be a highlight for her, too. He would make this momentous occasion last as long as possible.

Slowly drawing one spaghetti strap off her shoulder, then the other, he revealed, inch by inch, her full, pale breasts and the pink buds that crowned them. "You're so beautiful."

Her dubious smile melted him.

With his tongue, he proceeded to flick her pearled nipples, each in turn, before sucking gently, persistently, until her quick, indrawn breaths turned to whimpers.

Then he moved languorously down the length of her lithe body, performing a thorough reconnaissance of her perfect form by taking in every curve and hollow he came across.

By the time he'd nibbled his way from the backs of her knees to her inner thighs, Maya's skin burned like hot silk beneath his lips. He lifted the hem of her teddy, following its ascension toward the warm mystery between her legs. She parted them while sending him a look of such carnal anticipation that he could not deny her.

He buried his face in her golden curls like a starving man who'd finally found a feast. Trying to ease her yearning without pushing her over the edge too soon, he parted her sensual, swollen lips, sought and found the heart of her pleasure, and lightly blew on it. She bucked under him, and he smiled, feeling the answering throb of his own need.

Neither of them was going to last long—at least, not the first time.

Deftly he circled her pink nubbin with the pad of his thumb, watching her response. Her eyes melted shut. The tip of her tongue appeared to wet her slightly parted lips.

Rusty lowered his head and replaced his thumb with his tongue.

Her moan of approval made him smile again. Inhaling her sweet woman's musk, he devoted himself to finding out what pleased her most—flicking her lightly while stroking two fingers inside of her silky-slick opening.

Her thighs trembled as she strained toward his touch. He would have been content to pleasure her that way for as long as it took, when she suddenly sank her fingers into the hair on his head and issued a keening cry that brought the dog running toward their closed door. Her hips bucked and her inner muscles clenched his fingers.

"Oh, my God," she breathed as the paroxysm

faded. Her eyes drifted open and she regarded him in wonder as he lifted his head. "I totally forgot how amazing that could feel."

Tamping down his ridiculous pride, he grinned as he clambered up and over her, holding himself there so she could absorb the full impact of her effect on him. "I'll remind you any time you want," he promised.

Her gaze touched him like a warm caress as she took in the breadth of his chest, following the line of tawny hair that arrowed toward the band of his boxer briefs and then the head of his sex peeking out of the slit at the front.

To his gratification, she slipped her hand through the opening to encircle him. A growl of anticipation rumbled in his chest and his jaw clenched as he moved within her hold.

"I want to feel you inside me," she admitted. "Now."

"My lady gets what she wants, whenever it's within my power." He hustled to remove his underwear, not sure where they landed when he tossed them behind him. Then, starting with a kiss, he penetrated her, slowly, carefully, joining their bodies with a sense of awe he doubted he would ever grow immune to.

As he'd predicted, their first joining was not a marathon, more like an incredibly satisfying sprint.

Between the warm welcome of her silken passage and his galloping enthusiasm, he struggled to hang on, feeling as green as a teen having sex for the first time.

Maya pressed closer, her pillows tumbling to the floor. He surged into her, taking as much pleasure from her grasping inner muscles as from her small cries of satisfaction. Only when she seemed to melt around him did he let go, his release coming like an unstoppable train on the tracks.

At last, he came to rest with his face buried in her hair, his heart thudding against hers. Exhaustion broke over him without warning. It was all he could do to withdraw from her before he slipped into a warm tide of unconsciousness. He forced himself to roll out of bed and wash up.

By the time he returned from a quick visit to the bathroom and rejoined her in the bed, pulling her limp body into his embrace, she was sound asleep...with what looked to be a smile on her face.

Rusty closed his heavy eyes and sighed. Never in a million years could he have predicted the way his date would play out. Highs and lows included, he wouldn't change one thing about the way it had all fallen into place.

EPILOGUE

"**Y**OU DON'T NEED to be nervous," Maya reassured her son as she, Curtis, and Rusty sat outside the military judge's chambers, waiting for Curtis to be called to provide his testimony.

The case against Goddard, Smith, and Lubber had proceeded beyond an Article 32 hearing to a full-blown court-martial. In deference to Curtis's tender age, he had been summoned to testify before the judge and the JAG officers only. The judge would fill in the jury later, and the accused would never even lay eyes on him.

"I'm not nervous," Curtis insisted, then promptly belied his statement by wiping his palms on his dress pants.

Maya and Rusty shared a look.

She tried again. "Will Goddard is looking at ten years in jail, at a minimum. Even if he managed to send someone in his place to get back at you, they would never find you."

They had moved out to Never Forget Retreat on July Fourth, just in time to shoot off dozens of celebratory fireworks.

Curtis sat back with a laugh. "I hope he tries." He looked over at Rusty and shook his head. "Good luck getting past Draco and my stepdad."

Maya hid a smile. She and Rusty weren't married yet—they'd planned a fall wedding—but Curtis had obviously taken to the idea of having a SEAL for a stepfather, although he'd made it clear he was going to be a Marine dog handler when he grew up.

"So, you'll just go in there and tell the judge what happened, and that's that," she said.

"Mom, I'm okay. I'm just worried about leaving Draco by himself for so long."

"Oh," she said, nodding and meeting Rusty's twinkling gaze again.

Suddenly, the door to the judge's chambers opened and out stepped Santana, looking surprisingly clean-cut in a button-up shirt and slacks that had probably belonged to his father. He met Curtis's expectant gaze and grimaced.

Curtis stood up suddenly and made his way over to him. Maya watched as they exchanged a handclasp and a few words. She had heard that Santana and his mother had taken Will Goddard's threats seriously and, with the help of the U.S. Marshall

Service Witness Security Program, they were moving out of state.

This was goodbye for the two friends. Maya still didn't appreciate Santana for embroiling her son in his uncle's criminal life, but she had thanked him personally for having the courage to do the right thing, to show them where Curtis had been imprisoned, and to testify against his uncle.

"Bye, Santana," she called as he headed for his mother who at that moment stepped out of the ladies' room.

The JAG waiting at the door cleared his throat. "The judge is waiting, Curtis."

Maya resisted the urge to usher her son into the room while whispering last-minute advice in his ear. Instead, she threaded her fingers through Rusty's, closed her eyes, and willed this ordeal to be over soon.

Thank God Rusty is in my life. As the thought rippled through her head, she realized it had replaced the mantra, *If only Ian were still alive.*

"Are you going to miss this?" he asked, shifting closer and putting an arm around her shoulders.

Two weeks ago, she had given NCIS notice she would be leaving her post as special investigator. After fifteen years of ferreting out criminals, the time had come to do something more uplifting with her time. Helping to run a non-profit that improved the lives of special operators was proving far more satisfying, and Rusty had even offered to pay her to offset the loss of her income. While she helped Rusty maintain the retreat, at the same time raising money and awareness, Curtis cut grass on the riding lawnmower and put up with Draco in his bed. Life was a dream.

"Not at all," she answered truthfully. She sent him a smile. "I know you have a lot to do back home. Thanks for coming this morning."

He squeezed her hand. "Family comes first."

She searched his dear, rugged face. "We're not married yet."

He shrugged. "That's a formality. Family is a feeling."

Apparently those vows whispered in the aftermath of lovemaking were what really counted. They had sworn to love each other forever, to raise Curtis to be hardworking, honest, and patriotic. Maybe Rusty's visions of ghosts were like feelings—you couldn't see them or examine them, but they existed, nonetheless.

"You're right," she agreed, leaning closer to kiss him. "Family is a feeling."

ACKNOWLEDGMENTS

I am so privileged to be surrounded by loyal readers and talented friends. Without their helps my stories would fall far short of gratifying those who read them. My deepest thanks goes to my beta readers, Joyce, Penny, Pam, and Elizabeth. Thank you to Wendie for brainstorming with me at the beginning and to Suzanne for your professional final edit. All of these ladies are amazing. As for my best friend and developmental editor, Sydney Jane Baily—there's no one in the world who could take your place. As we say here in Virginia, y'all are the best!

OTHER BOOKS BY
MARLISS MELTON

ECHO PLATOON SERIES
LOOK AGAIN (Novella #1)
DANGER CLOSE
HARD LANDING
FRIENDLY FIRE
HOT TARGET (coming 2017)

TASKFORCE SERIES
THE PROTECTOR
THE GUARDIAN
THE ENFORCER

NAVY SEAL TEAM 12 SERIES
FORGET ME NOT
IN THE DARK
TIME TO RUN
NEXT TO DIE
CODE OF SILENCE, a novella
TOO FAR GONE
LONG GONE, a novella
SHOW NO FEAR

Made in United States
Orlando, FL
24 May 2023

33444430R00114